I0733809

Antifa Lit Journal

Volume 1:

What If We Kissed While Sinking a Billionaire's Yacht?

by

Rachel A. Rosen - Casey Aimer
Kent Karnofski - Benjamin Gorman
Joanna Michal Hoyt - Julia Figliotti
A.M. Pennyfeather - Brian U. Garrison
Christopher Scott Thompson
Trixie Belka - Stephanie Carrier-Boodram
J.L. Henker - Madeline White
M. K. Martin - Desiree Batiste
Rick M. Cook - Karen Eisenbrey
John Slovacek - Jes Honard

Introduction by Chrys Gorman

Published in the United States by
Not a Pipe Publishing Ink-Corporated, LLC
Independence, Oregon.
www.NotAPipePublishing.com

Paperback Edition

ISBN-13: 978-1-956892-64-2

Cover by Rachel A. Rosen

Contents

Introduction

by Chrys Gorman

How did I find myself in Barcelona, Spain, sitting on my apartment rooftop, reading submissions for an antifascist anthology, choosing which works should be included, which poems speak to the soul of a person living through a fascist regime? What right do I have to judge the words of authors infinitely more talented than myself?

I am acutely cognizant of my own privileged upbringing, raised upper-middle class, white, and cisgender in the "greatest country in the world." But also, queer, disabled, neurodivergent, and raised by a narcissistic, emotionally abusive mother and an alcoholic father. So, while I have no particular qualifications to judge great works of literary talent, I do have an intimate knowledge of a lifetime of living under the weight of a society that seeks to crush, exploit, humiliate, control, and oppress those who are 'other.'

My personality is best reflected by Elizabeth Bennet, the "obstinate, headstrong girl" from my favorite book, Jane Austen's *Pride and Prejudice*. Much like Miss Bennet, "There is a stubbornness about me that never can bear to be frightened at the will of others. My courage always rises at every attempt to intimidate me." My idols were found in strong female authors' works, women who refused to bend to the will of men, who refused to subvert themselves for the 'greater good' of an uninformed society. For inspiration, I look to the iconic Maya Angelou:

> "A bird that stalks
> down his narrow cage
> can seldom see through
> his bars of rage
> his wings are clipped and
> his feet are tied
> so he opens his throat to sing."

So why am I sitting here, 4,000 miles from the country of my birth, evaluating the merits of the works of current authors? The answer is so simple, yet oh-so-complicated. I married a publisher. An author. A teacher. An activist. We stood on street corners holding "Black Lives Matter" signs, we published an anthology of exclusively queer voices, and we proudly hung Harris/Walz 2024 signs in our front yard. We built a wonderful life together. He stood by my side every time I climbed on my soapbox, wearing my ever-present guillotine earrings, and advocated for queer lives, for young girls who deserve a seat at the table, for overlooked and overcorrected neurodivergent children, for survivors of narcissistic parents and childhood trauma, for adoptees. I spoke out loudly, uncomfortably, and passionately for every silenced voice that I could.

And then Donald Trump was elected to a second term in office. So, we left. We packed, sold, and donated every aspect of our life, hopped on a plane, and started to rebuild in Spain. See? Simple, right? How could I stay when I no longer believed that America was worth fighting for? I was never a great patriot; I've always believed in the people, not the place. But in those months between Election Night and Inauguration Day, I found myself existing in a constant state of fear. Far too many of my neighbors believed that my life did not matter, that the lives of our fellow human beings did not matter. I've lost my faith in America, and in far too many Americans.

But I still believe in the power of our voices, in the strength of literature, in the community of the written word. Voices matter. Stories matter. Words are timeless and infinitely powerful. As Charlotte Brontë writes in *Jane Eyre*: "I am no bird, and no net ensnares me; I am a free human being with an independent will." Perhaps publishing this anthology is my way of regaining a little bit of my faith in my fellow human beings. At a time when oligarchs and politicians are trying to divide us, to scare us, to silence us, it's more important than ever to speak up. Even when it sometimes feels like screaming into the void.

So, keep writing and keep reading. We are the keepers of history. America may descend further into fascism, fear and hopelessness may spread, and this fight may take generations to win, but remember, as Ursula K. LeGuin writes in *The Left Hand of Darkness*: "One voice speaking truth is a greater force than fleets and armies..."

The moral arc of the universe is bending towards fascism. I refuse to be cowed into silence. And Not a Pipe Publishing will always stand for diversity, equity, inclusion, and accessibility. We understand how much courage it takes an author to speak out in the face of an administration that uses fear to silence those who oppose them. We are proud to introduce Volume 1 of the *Antifa Lit Journal*. We are deeply grateful for your support, and we hope you enjoy this collection.

-Chrys Gorman
8th of April 2025

What If We Kissed While Sinking a Billionaire's Yacht?

by Rachel A. Rosen

Something is wrong with the water. It's not your fault that you can't identify that something. Your brain evolved for herring and song, not the wanton desecration of the only known habitable planet.

It's not just the faint chemical tang at the back of your tongue, nor the silt particles suspended for longer than they should be, turning the sweetness to grit in your mouth. It is the vibration, distant still, drilling into your otic capsule. The ocean is restless. Wounded. It churns in the wake of an incursion, even as it slicks smooth against your skin in apology.

You had just about decided to put it out of your mind, as the Matriarch commanded. You had resigned yourself to the mysteries of the World Above as surely as you resigned yourself to those of the World Below, of the Midnight and the Abyss, the forbidden places that squeeze flesh to bone. The sky holds wonders and terrors beyond your comprehension, and to dwell on them is to forgo the worldly pleasures of a writhing salmon crushed between your jaws, or the ripple of sun-dappled water upon your back. You have all you want, here in the Sunlight Zone, and know all you need.

And so, you too might have slowly become accustomed to the change in the water, the way everything contracts and withers and fades with the passage of time, were it not for Ula.

Ula, the new whale, has seen something like this before. She came up from the Mediterranean with her fins scarred and new clicks and whistles in her vocabulary. For days she has insisted that your pod address this threat, but the Matriarch is focused on pursuing a harem of seals that has abruptly turned west. She doesn't care about Ula or her scars, or why she has trailed your pod for weeks, pursuing silently until her call alerted you to her presence.

My apologies: Her name isn't Ula any more than yours is Yoka. Our language of arcane symbols does your language violence. But if I am to convey your story to a human readership, it is a blow I must strike. I'm trying for sensitivity here. There's a greater good. You are free to disagree.

Ula, then, is beautiful. She is older than you, and she has seen more. Your language has a thousand words for the minute differences in current and eddy, but none for the map of ridged skin across her fin, the mismatch between upper and lower jaw that turns her smile cruel and clever.

Her people's knowledge is conveyed in these new, foreign sounds. They have learned to fight back. They know the vulnerabilities of the invader, the places where its cold flesh is weakest. The alternative is death.

The Matriarch won't listen, but you do.

Maria calculates trajectories like a pool player lines up a shot or a forensics team examines a murder, but she can't figure out how the shit got all the way up under there. She almost failed Physics, so what does she know, but it doesn't really seem possible. The guests' coke must be spiked with laxatives because no one can shit that much, not even the rich, who do everything in excess.

It looks liquidy but it's stubborn, like it's baked right into the porcelain. Splashed up inside the rim, Jackson Pollock style. She didn't almost fail Art. That's why she's working for minimum wage on this floating hellscape, not off being an astronaut or a Wall St. banker. The shitter made a hundred times her salary while he was letting loose that spray. The human body is a marvel, and Maria is exhausted and wants to sleep forever.

The royalty partying on the *Galbraith* don't seem to sleep at all, not that it slows them down. They're living their best lives nonstop: mimosas in the morning, molly by night, pretend-happy—maybe even real happy sometimes—once the euphoria hits. They've had their souls surgically removed and replaced with a hedge-fund portfolio, so who the fuck knows what passes for happy behind their dead eyes.

Maria scrubs at the shit stain with the brush until her hand cramps, until the last little dot vanishes, leaving gleaming porcelain, and she doesn't cry. She's 200 miles out from her grandmother's mofongo, a good book, or a sympathetic ear.

"You're three rooms behind," Grace shouts out.

"You wanna see what they left in there?" Maria yells at her supervisor's retreating broad back.

"Cry me a river, gorgeous. Cabin Five flushed a turd the size of my forearm. Or tried to. You think you got problems? Keep up."

Maria tries, moving on to the next door and whatever lurks behind it. There are worse stories. In one of the storage closets, there's a safety binder that no one ever checks, except to add to the sheet of lined paper a list of horrors the workers have come across on the yacht. Butt plugs, a brick of coke, a blow-up doll with Hilary Clinton's face. Someone claims to have found a fetus, but its veracity is debated in the page's marginalia.

She opens the next door without checking more than the room service notice, bustles in with her cleaning caddy, and goes right to work. When the shuffle of linen alerts her that she's not alone in the room, it's understandable that she shrieks.

A greener worker might mistake his clothes for casual. White linen shirt, open at the collarbone, blue jeans faded at the knee. Barefoot, rendering him curiously vulnerable. The prince of the floating palace isn't hideous.

"Sorry... sorry!" She backs away so quickly that she slams her hip into the caddy. His answering smile is broad, teeth like soldiers on parade. She turns to leave, but he crosses the cabin in three long strides.

"Wait. Do you know who I am?"

She nods. "Chase Braxton. CEO of BlueSpace Inc., Forbes Top 30 under 30. Everyone knows."

He gestures expansively to a drink cart by the wall. "What's your poison?"

It's all an elaborate trick to get her fired. Or worse. Maria looks past him, to the bed, both sides rumpled. "I'm working," she says. "Sir."

"And I own the *Galbraith*," he replies. This time, he doesn't bother to ask about her preferences but pours them each three fingers of a scotch she's pretty sure she couldn't have bought with a year's salary. "Stay awhile."

Because, Ula says, the Ones from the Sky are deadly in ways both overt and subtle, you must commit your body to total and perpetual war against them. There is room for you and the Blue People, though you sometimes fight and even kill them; there is room for you and the Many-Armed Ones and the Nautilus and the toothed things and the stinging things. The Sky Ones descend with bladed armor that can slice and spill your blood and blubber and soul to the ocean. You are fast and smart enough to evade their weapons and their direct attacks. It is the sly deaths they bring, the changes they weave in salt and spume, the great oily void of their wake.

Bera is laden with calf and her swim is heavy, held aloft more by the current of the pod than her own momentum. She cries softly and sings to the unborn calf. The other whales circle.

Few creatures would attack one of your kind, but a pregnant whale is vulnerable, her newborn calf soft and blind and trusting. You and Ula draw tight to her. You are keenly aware of your own body, its urges and will to survive, but it is the small, slick burden in Bera's belly that is your future. You guard it. Ula is wary, swimming farther from the pod and breaching more frequently. Later, you'll ask her if she knew what was to come, but she never gives a satisfying answer.

Instead, she tastes the ocean, the salt-fine air. The Sky One is closer. You strain to match her senses, but there is no glitter of distant white armor.

Nonetheless, you tell her that you believe her.

Maria gets invited to a party.

She gets a few precious hours to herself, time in which to shower, and sleep, and gobble down scraps from the banquet table. They have to share rooms, sleeping in shifts so that someone is always available to clean up a spill, and the space on the yacht is allotted with efficiency, maximizing the cabin's luxury and minimizing the staff's visibility. She packed light—two uniforms, which she alternates between, several pairs of shorts, and a few crumpled t-shirts. She has nothing to wear to a party with the ocean's elite, and it means forgoing her six hours of rest.

It's not, she rationalizes, because Chase is charming. Chase is like every fuckboy she's ever met except none of them owned a luxury yacht.

In the end, she borrows her roommate Susan's dress. It's a little baggy on her so she cinches it up with a knot of dental floss and hopes for the best.

Chase must have told her the wrong time because the party is in full swing on deck by the time she arrives. She's underdressed in the ill-fitting cotton number. The women are tall, bedazzled in shimmering cocktail dresses, every quirk of genetics smoothed out by contouring and plastic surgery. To Maria's bleary eyes, they're angels, the toes of their stiletto heels barely deigning to make contact with the deck.

LEDs in magenta and sapphire shimmer across the pool in time to the beat of the electro-pop soundtrack. Chase is sprawled at one end, one hand holding a cocktail and the other brushing the bare shoulder of an ethereal blond woman.

"Maria!" She doesn't remember telling him her name, but he's a genius, isn't he? He invented BlueSpace

AI, some kind of tool for analyzing stock market trends, or maximizing warehouse efficiency, military logistics, or, fuck, she doesn't really know, just that he's rich and works in tech and is therefore brilliant. Maybe he did bother to learn the names of his staff.

He motions her over and she immediately worries that there's still shit in her hair. "Someone, get this girl a drink."

He doesn't need to signal a particular stew. His wishes are granted out of the ether, and she's handed some kind of fancy martini with little gold flakes in it. Chase splashes the surface of the pool, sending peacock ripples over the water and eliciting an unhappy yelp from his companion.

"C'mon in."

"I don't have a bathing suit," Maria protests.

"Oh, oh, that's fine, uh—someone get this girl a bathing suit! You could, look here, just come over for a second—"

He grabs her arm and all but flings her into the pool. Maria shrieks, and several of Chase's guests, including the blond woman, laugh. The water is warmer than the night air. She hopes it's not chlorinated, or Susan's going to murder her for wrecking the dress.

"Relax, babe." A steel-haired man with a Botox-blank face splashes her. Her mouth is still parted, and she tastes the spray before she can close it. "Where'd you find this one, Braxton?"

"She's a stew," Chase says, and pauses, no doubt to mull over whether a cleaner counts as a stew. A deckie?

Or something lower, something beneath role and gender? "She cleans up your shit, Brooks. Show some respect."

"A *maid*!" The blond woman squeals, and Maria is no longer a beast beneath notice but something exotic, an alien whose descent signals a reordering of the cosmos.

"Pretty," another man observes.

"I only hire pretty ones." Chase removes his arm from the woman and slides an ass-width closer to Maria. She stiffens. It could be friendly, even protective. All their eyes are on her.

His body—startlingly well-built for someone who spends his days in office boardrooms and treating high-profile clients to three-martini lunches—shields her from at least some of them.

But she's not naïve. She knows where this is probably heading. "No" is not among the range of permissible answers.

She's mercifully spared by the intrusion of Captain Hart, his crisp whites oddly formal amongst the pool of partygoers. He leans and whispers something to Chase that Maria only catches snippets of. *Turn* and *conditions* and *risk*.

Chase laughs, abrupt and overloud. "*Whales*!" he shouts.

"Sir." But the genie's been uncorked and decanted, and the captain's attempt at discretion has been thwarted.

"Captain Hart here says there's *whales* nearby."

"Orcas," Hart specifies. "A pod of them. We have no

reason to believe they're a danger to the ship, but just in case, it's advisable to reroute. It should only add an hour onto the itinerary."

"I want to see the whales!" The woman's voice rises another half-tone.

"There you have it." Chase beams his military parade of a smile at the captain. "The lady wants to see some whales. Stay the course."

Bera's birth is prolonged. She sings through her pain. Her call draws sharks, alight and alert at the prospect of blood.

After long hours, the fan of the calf's tail emerges. Bera corkscrews through the water and keens, slowing to the barest motion. The tail, a small mirror to her own, flaps weakly.

You exchange low, worried clicks with Ula, but you mustn't speak, mustn't stoke the fears of the pod or alert the sharks, though they must know what no one in the pod will admit.

There is still a chance that the calf slides free. You can't give up hope.

It emerges in a black burst and a fountain of blood. And, indeed, there is a brief moment where the calf twitches, where you can pretend. But its spine is bent, a tormented loop that twists its head nearly backward. Its lungs are underdeveloped, taking on water as it spirals, propelled by its malformed body to drowning depths.

Bera pushes it up to no avail.

It cries the entire time it dies.

Bera floats in the wake of the pod, the corpse of her calf bobbing beside her, carried by the current. Only when it drifts does she at last force herself to move, corralling it to her side.

Her calls are low and keening, and you will not allow them to break you, not when Ula is right, not when there is revenge to be taken for this.

You wait until the resting line has formed, most of the pod logged by the surface in unihemispheric sleep to follow Ula when she breaks from the others, into the navy depths.

The blond—Bryana, she specifies it's with a Y, and Maria spends long minutes trying to figure out where the Y goes—hangs off the prow of the yacht. She's pretending to be Rose from Titanic when someone spots the whales off the starboard. Maria can't help herself and she joins the rush to the side. In the murky violet haze before dawn, the dark shapes might be some less-exciting fish, or ocean junk. But when Captain Hart steers the ship in an arc towards the whales, she catches the telltale black fins knifing through the surface.

She has seen Marineland commercials, *Blue Planet* episodes, but 4K resolution misses the alien synchronicity of the whales' dance. Maria leans over the railing, straining to catch a glimpse of a black, glistening eye on a white ovoid, the eruption of a blowhole. But the whales avoid the yacht's passage, and the vessel is too large and ungainly for Hart to follow them.

"I'm king of the world!" Bryana shrieks before joining them.

Brooks wraps an arm around Maria's waist. He's ugly-drunk, his breath warm and sour against her cheek. "Want to see a bigger whale?" he whispers.

"Don't be disgusting." It's Chase, coming up behind them. Chastened, Brooks removes the offending arm and backs off. It's almost impressive, the two alpha fuckboys facing off over her, except that the seductive depths of the ocean are more appealing than physical contact with either of them. A mental stream of David Attenborough narration carries her through the awkwardness: *Here, the larger of the two apex predators demonstrates his dominance by flashing his Rolex, but that may not be enough to convince a female to mate with him.* "Bryana was asking where you went," Chase says to Brooks smoothly.

How can she be as tired as she is and keep moving? Only the railing and the excitement of the whales—maybe the pill she unwisely popped when they were poolside—keep her upright.

"You're too smart and pretty to be cleaning toilets," he says.

She's not quite smart enough to stop herself from saying, "My father didn't own a uranium mine in Namibia, and college doesn't come cheap."

She is, however, pretty enough to carry it off, because

he laughs. "There are better ways to fund an education."

He edges closer, his perfectly manicured hand inches from where hers grips the railing.

It's going to happen, she knows it's going to happen, but the moment lurches forward as slowly as its trajectory is inevitable.

"I could help you," Chase says. The ship lurches, too, idly flicked by an invisible hand.

He can rescue a hundred, a thousand talented working-class girls in the time between his first coffee and his first martini lunch. It would barely make a scratch in his annual dividends. He could have financed polio eradication or run her entire state on solar generators, but instead he's grinning wolfishly at her, his beautiful hand sidling ever closer to hers.

She knows all about deals with the Devil. None of the heroes in those stories ever had to clean up billionaire's shit from underneath a toilet seat.

She waits for too long. "You can think on it," he says. "I would never dream of pressuring you."

"Chase!" Bryana-with-a-Y shrieks. The delight has been violently stripped from her voice. Chase races to the bridge deck, and Maria follows him.

There's a man in the water. It's a long way down from the deck of the yacht. The pale, floundering shape might be another log or ocean flotsam, but then it starfishes, and she can make the limbs out clearly.

"It's Brooks," Bryana says. "He lost his balance on the edge, and—"

The remaining partygoers helplessly fail to drop the

lifeboat, so Maria runs for the life preserver she saw on the swim platform. It's heavy and the martinis have turned her arms to limp noodles, so when she casts it off the side, it skips across the surface and bumps a wave to land a few feet from the hull, yards from where Brooks flounders. "Swim!" she screams out, though if that were an option, surely he'd have done it. The wave splashes over the deck. All she can see is blinding white.

Chase is reaching for her from the main deck, flattened on the outcropping. She swings loose from the ladder, and he catches her under the arms, hauls her up into a muscular embrace.

When she blinks her eyes clear, she can still see Brooks, a tiny speck in the boat's wake.

She huddles in a chilled little ball. Chase speed dials his lawyer, and Maria cycles through fantasies where she enacted a heroic rescue, or where she never signed on to the boat at all.

"Go on to my cabin," he tells her. He's too important to be put on hold at 4 a.m.; she can hear the lawyer through the tinny speaker. "You can use my shower. I'll be there soon."

Numb, her hands and feet balloon-thick and unwieldy, she trudges to obey him.

The tiny Sky One squirms like a salmon, but not for very long.

You have mostly eaten fish and seals, easy, nutritious

prey, but not much of a challenge.

You have even eaten shark. There is a novelty to it, devouring the heart and guts of a creature that, on its own, might have been your match. Your hunt is more powerful with Ula.

You taste the new prey from Ula's own mouth. The meat is not so soft as a seal's, but it tears pleasantly between your jaws. She insists that the two of you can flense loose the fins of the big Sky One. She promises more, and sweeter meat, within.

The pod is not very far off, and you could still turn back, but how could you turn back when Ula is there, scarred and graceful and dappled in the thin streaks of starlight that bleed into the shallows? You could no more leave her than you could have abandoned Bera in her time of need.

Ula calls to the pod, notes of grief and revenge and, most of all, of harvest. You echo, the creature's rich blood still wet on your tongue. Silence greets you both. They won't leave Bera, or they have abandoned you to your quixotic quest.

Ula promises that it will only take two of you. The others will hear. The others will follow.

Such endeavours, such moments of rupture, must always begin with someone.

Even with the shower scalding Maria's skin, the heat fails to penetrate. Her bones are cold, her organs dense and heavy, encased in ice. She takes longer than she should—any moment Chase will come back, any moment she'll see just how much of her frozen soul she can surrender. At last, she emerges in a towel. Her borrowed dress is still on the floor, but she can't bear to smell it, and it's all wet. She stumbles through the cabin in search of anything that might fit.

There's a sweater that comes down to her knees, and a pair of jeans that work if she rolls up the cuffs. He's only going to undress her anyway. At least he's hot. There are probably women who'd kill for the opportunity.

Where is he? She imagines him consoling his distraught guests, or breaking news of Brooks' death to his family. Maybe that's what he's doing. Her bare feet are cold on the tiled floor.

Maybe he'll have a bra from one of his earlier conquests lying around, and while it might not be clean, at least it'd be dry. Anyway, that's the excuse that has her at his desk, and once she's there, she can't help but peek. Investments, donations, a photo of him and the president. A white paper outlining a new application. Who wouldn't look? A normal life doesn't include people like Chase. Fairy tale princes pulling drowning working girls from the ocean, promising riches and paid-off student debts.

The door opens.

She closes the folder, not quickly enough. The disgust must show on her face, the illusion of the innocent naif to be swept onto his luxurious bed shattering before his eyes.

"I need to go," she says.

"Where?" His voice is still playful, despite his soulless shark eyes. "Into the ocean with Brooks?"

"I'm sorry," Maria tells him. "I didn't mean to look, I really didn't, I—"

"You can look," he says lightly, like none of it matters. "That's some of my best work."

The cabin no longer feels so expansive. There's whisky on his breath.

"AI profiling software?" She's always had a vision of herself as the type of person who stands up to injustice, but now all she can do is look for an escape route.

"It's a dangerous world out there," Chase says.

"I've heard about that stuff," she says. "It's janky. It… it flags anyone darker than a paper bag as an illegal and dumps them into camps. People like me."

She hadn't expected a laugh. "I'm being lectured on my business decisions by the help now?"

A rabbit in a snare, Maria backs up as far as her chain will allow her, lower back colliding with the desk and ruffling the papers.

"There are innocent people, children, even. How can you—"

"Because it's the zeitgeist. It's securing the future—for *our* children. You think you understand innovation? Because, what, you've had a year or two wasting your money at some liberal college? You clean up *shit*."

She runs. It's stupid, it's useless, but she feints and dodges past him through the door, still clutching the white paper, a wild break for freedom. There is nothing between her and the ocean but the railing, and she casts his atrocities into the water.

He's behind her, and suddenly the ocean feels safer.

She hasn't prayed in years, and now, when she does, it isn't to God.

When the yacht pitches violently to the starboard side, throwing her like a rag doll against the wall of the cabin, she thinks, of all the fucking prayers to get answered.

Your jaws have rent whale flesh from bone, but the skin of the Sky One is harder than rock. Ula, between lunges and snaps, urges you to push, and you throw your weight at it. It is as big as an iceberg, and it resists you.

The creature is greater than you, greater than Ula, more deadly than the combined predation of the pod, but you could never surrender to it. It heaves, and its great fin groans and screams. One fin catches your side as it snaps, the pain like a shark's bite, but you shove at its upside-down spine, fury streaming through the waves to tangle with your blood.

Maria scrambles after Chase as he screams orders to Captain Hart. They're taking on water fast; the sea has turned traitor on them, the yacht rocked from side to side like a child's toy in a storm drain. There's cold water up to her shins now. Chase berates the crew, but it won't help. They can't turn fast enough. The yacht, top of the line, shining white as a glacier and sleek as a shark, isn't nimble enough to dodge whatever lurks below the surface.

She runs, bare feet sliding on the slick deck, to fling her arms around the railing on the port side. The ship gives another pained lurch, but she's up high now. Someone's in the water, white bodies thrashing and flailing. Chase can surveil the entire world and raise the stock exchange to the heavens but here, tossed in churning waters, the plaything of an unseen enemy, at last his voice falters.

The ship is pulled downwards, and there's a crack, and Maria screws her eyes shut and screams and screams. The last thing she'll see is the wave bearing down on them. The last thing she'll taste is the salt burning her nostrils, filling her mouth.

He's still calling her—Maria, this time, Maria Maria, and she sees that Chase has somehow slipped down to the ruin of the lower deck, clinging to a broken ledge of wood against a wave that threatens to drag him out. She's just above him. He swings a hand upwards, pale fingers extending towards her, and if she leaned out just a little more, she could maybe grab it, maybe haul him up towards the part of the ship that's still mostly above water, if he didn't drag her down with him.

And she almost does that.

Mere yards from the boat, first one orca breaches,

then a second, arcing and then diving low to shove at the yacht's keel. Their black and white is mesmerizing, and they're glossy as a Lisa Frank drawing in the moonlight. They're so close. She's transfixed and Chase is still yelling, cursing her now, calling her a bitch and a wetback, and then his words dissolve into the ocean's roar.

She doesn't see the moment where his hands detach from the wreckage of the ship, nor the instant where the dark water carries him under. It all happens so much faster than she would have expected. Later, when the rescuers arrive, she'll think it's almost fitting: Move fast and break people.

Maria faints. You can't stay conscious in water that cold, not after a night that's been a Rube Goldberg device of trauma, and of course she's shaken, babbling hysterically when they find her. Which means that no one can be sure if it's true, that last thing she remembers seeing.

No one but Maria, who sees the whales dance, nearly entwined, splashing and leaping in waters too dark to distinguish them from the stelliferous night. The billionaire is tugged between the two orcas' powerful jaws like the spaghetti in *Lady and the Tramp*. Above the storm, above the groan of metal, ringing in her ears until the day she dies, is the alien triumph of whalesong.

You love her.

The understanding comes in a flash of red, in salt and fat and gristle, in the kick and twitch of the meat in your jaws and the tender brush of fin against fin. You love her—not as a pod mate or a sister but as a companion. You have swum together for days, long enough to court a mate, but it is only now that you realize that this is what Ula has been doing the entire time.

The warrior's defeated prey floats around her, streaks of blood lifting from her white line of sharp teeth to dissolve into the ocean. Her black eyes gleam. She circles you again, and you click and clap your jaw. You breach together, splashing, before diving low. She nips playfully at your tongue. You twine with her.

When you rejoin the pod, the harvest from the Sky One will feed them for days. The pod will feast and forgive your rebellion.

Ula rejoices in the hunt you shared, but she bears the scars of other Sky Ones. There will be more. They will come, and keep coming, with their cruel blades and their poisoned wake.

You promise her this: When they do, you and she will feast again.

Politics of Stolen Body Parts

by Casey Aimer

I'm recycled against my will each evening
as a walking election billboard, shoved out
lumbering through downtown streets to lie
how this month's politician will save anyone.

My mouth is always stolen first.

This voice I swing is threatening, but
words are weak and easily silenced.

Rival factions relentlessly steal pieces
of me, violently ending programmed
propaganda to control the message
as if their actions will censor me.

Next they yank my head, but it's bolted

on a neck that hasn't learned to revolt.

Failure makes them angrier, mob me
until my fingers are removed, peeled
individually away to stop me miming
alongside these ads in sign language.

But these hands sans fingers
are still bludgeoning risks so
stumps are left alone—too sad,
useless for pointed retribution.

Both legs are sawed off with a Dremel
along my thighline, stopping mobile ads,
fastening me to where I am already—
in-between neon signs barely bathed
in light, existing as flimsy reflectors.

Robot eyes are kept whole and online
because they want my owners to see
this happening—all I am reduced to—
dying messenger pigeon on its last flight.

They save my chest cavity for last, graffitied
or painted blank gray—as if humans know
to save the heartful killing blow for last.

If I could speak, I'd have agreed with them:

Keep stealing me.

I want to send a message to my owners, too.

Night School

by Kent Karnofski

The spotlight loops around me, and I crouch behind a tree. I try to be patient, but I'm late and the others will worry. The moon provides only a crescent of light, but my eyes have adjusted, and I know my way through the woods. The old high school is faintly visible now. I'm close.

I wait for the light to pass once more, then scurry through darkness, through the underbrush, to the other side of the brick wall. Now, I can walk upright. The door is propped open, and I walk down the hall.

Grandpop told me about when he was in school here, how proud the students were with their new building: marble floors, wood trimming, the front promenade. The bell tower. It was a beautiful place. Before. Now vacant, abandoned, neglected, shunned.

Nearly forgotten.

Except by a few of us.

I carefully descend the dark staircase to the basement–Grandpop said he took typing down here–and I enter our room. My comrades are huddled around a dim lantern. A couple of them have flashlights. I count five, and I'm six. All present.

"Did you bring it?" Franklin asks.

"Hi, Fillmore, glad to see you. Do you have the book?" Jackson is more friendly in demeanor, but we are all savage to learn.

"I have it." I hold up *Calculus*.

"Great," said Mr. Hamilton. "Thank you, Fillmore. Tonight, we'll continue reading John Irving, then some chemistry, and finally another Calculus lesson."

Mr. Hamilton has been leading our studies for three years now. It's slow going. We only meet twice a week for three lessons per session, but we never take vacations.

Education is forbidden.

That's not true. The authorities discourage critical thinking.

A few public schools remain open–day schools. They are cruel and godly. *The Bible* is taught, and farming, cooking, and basic health. That's about it. Companies have on-the-job training, and everyone is expected to keep themselves healthy enough to work 60 hours a week, ergo health class. Calisthenics, hygiene, diet, stuff like that.

But a few of us try to learn what used to be freely encouraged. Literature and sciences. Mathematics. History.

We learn these things slowly, secretively, valiantly. If caught, Mr. Hamilton would receive prison time; my classmates and I would be shown the internment camp at the edge of town. It's exhausting, but we trudge on, believing our lives are better the more we learn. We are proud philomaths.

Tonight, we read from Irving's *Cider House Rules*. Because we have limited time, and only one copy of the book, Mr. Hamilton summarizes parts, and we read parts aloud. We skip through, and he fills in blanks. We typically complete one novel every three weeks.

After that, we talk through a chemistry experiment. The equipment to perform science experiments are still in the labs upstairs, but we don't have the power required, or gas for Bunsen burners, or the light to see by, so we talk through them. After we finish studying a concept, Mr. Hamilton describes the apparatus and the setup, and, as a group, we figure out what should happen and explain why.

Next is Calculus and after that discussion, we memorize a problem for homework.

The arc of a batted baseball is described by a parabola. Make assumptions and fit an equation for a ball hit to the outfield and caught 300 feet from home plate. At what distance from home plate is the baseball's velocity equal to zero?

Our next meeting is at the old data center, and we'll discuss methods of solution. We never use paper. Sometimes, if someone finds chalk, we can use the blackboard, then we're careful to erase everything.

It's time to go. Mr. Hamilton tells us to contemplate the ethics of truthfulness. We creep up the stairwell together, silently, then take turns departing into the lonely darkness. Before I leave, Jackson gives me a hug. She smells nice.

We each have pre-assigned routes to get home–mine takes me about fifty minutes. If I walked straight home, it would take, maybe, ten minutes, but that would be careless. I enter the woods to the south and slank along the riverbank until I cross the second walking bridge, then I backtrack and walk through the office park being reclaimed by the trees and the deer. Birds live there, too. Racoons.

I think about Jackson. I think I'll ask her to meet me somewhere. Like a date. Maybe. It doesn't even have to be private. Shoot, the authorities want us to hook up. Well, not so much hook up, but marry and have kids. Or get pregnant, have kids, get married. Whatever. The order of events doesn't seem important, as long as we achieve those goals. Anyway, I'm not so much thinking about having kids with Jackson as much as I think about her lips. We could go to town for ice cream.

I walk through an abandoned bookstore and down the dark alley to my back door. A few times now, the authorities have bothered Dad about the broken lights, and a utility worker once fixed them. In night school, we learned how to short out a circuit so that a repairman wouldn't know the difference between faulty parts or sabotage. This way, I have a better chance of getting home unseen.

My parents always wait up for me, worried what to do if I get caught after curfew. I ask Dad for $50 to take Jackson on a date. That's a lot of money, he says, handing over three twenties. He winks. I kiss Mom on the cheek and go to bed. I have time for a nap before sunrise.

At day school, Franklin walks up behind me and whispers, "Shibboleth," and keeps walking. That's our codeword that something went wrong, and night school is shut down. Probably just a scare. But maybe somebody was caught, or our stash of books was found.

We'll await a whispered "Ephraimites" to make the rounds, telling us to go back underground.

Ask the Pallbearer

by Benjamin Gorman

ask the pallbearer
the first heft
is most difficult
especially just
a bit too soon
when the others catch up
weight shared
not easy but
level as pressed lips
shaky as gritted teeth
a long march
too late to prevent tragedy
we can mourn together
and bury this

Those Who Mourn

by Joanna Michal Hoyt

Week 1

Jessie Bennet gripped her sign and tried to think less about how sweaty she was and more about why she was there.

Dolores' idea had sounded good at the women's Bible study. *Bear witness. Make them see the faces. Show them we remember*. When Ruth asked nervously whether that sort of thing was legal anymore, Beatrice reminded everyone of the executive order rooting out anti-Christian bias. *So, we'll all have Bible verses on our signs, and we'll quote Scripture and sing hymns, and Dawn will be filming if anyone gives us trouble, and you can bet your booty, she'll make them look bad...*

So here they were, thirteen tired women—too few to need a permit, even—wearing long black dresses on a muggy June afternoon that felt more like August. They stood on the sidewalk facing across the street toward their representative's district office, toward the American flag and the Trump flag out front. They waved their signs and were ignored. The representative wasn't there, of course. His staffers glanced nervously at the women but didn't stop to talk with them. A few cars honked: Support? Derision? The women were too hot and short of breath to sing hymns. Their representative said climate change was a hoax. He'd probably say the same thing about the stories of the people on the signs the women carried.

Across the top each sign read MOURN WITH THOSE WHO MOURN: ROMANS 12:15. Across the bottom, AS YOU DID IT TO ONE OF THE LEAST OF THESE MY BROTHERS AND SISTERS, YOU DID IT TO ME: MATTHEW 25:40. The middle of each sign showed a different face, a different story.

FERMIN ENRIQUEZ, 38, LIVED AND WORKED IN YOUR STATE 17 YEARS WHILE WAITING FOR A RULING ON HIS ASYLUM CASE. NO CRIMINAL RECORD. DEPORTED BY ICE. KILLED BY THE GANGS HE FLED. HE HAS THREE YOUNG CHILDREN.

(*That kind of thing has been happening for years*, Beatrice had pointed out. *It's not because of the election.* Dolores sighed. *You think I don't know that? I should have started doing this years ago. Maybe some of you would even have joined me then.* (How they'd all flinched at that...) *But better late than never. Anyway, it's been happening for years, but not to parents of kids from my day care. And who said this was all about the election?)*

SYLVIE PRICE, 15, DAUGHTER OF YOUR CONSTITUENTS. COMMITTED SUICIDE AFTER BEING KICKED OFF HER SPORTS TEAM, CONSISTENTLY CALLED A BOY, AND BULLIED BY PEOPLE ECHOING YOUR PRESIDENT'S LANGUAGE. THE CLUB THAT USED TO SUPPORT HER WAS DISBANDED AND THE TEACHER WHO USED TO HELP HER WAS FIRED.

SOCORRO DIAZ, 20, US CITIZEN, STUDENT AND COMMUNITY VOLUNTEER ARRESTED ILLEGALLY IN AN ICE RAID. NOBODY KNOWS WHERE SHE IS. INCLUDING HER PARENTS AND HER LITTLE SISTER.

ESME BOLLINGER, 42, YOUR CONSTITUENT, KILLED BY HER PARTNER AFTER HE WAS PARDONED FOR HIS ROLE IN THE JANUARY 6 TERROR ATTACK.

Dawn had worried aloud ahead of time about whether their group would get attacked for standing around with signs. Two hot hours later, as they put their signs back in the church van and drove home, Jessie wondered aloud whether being—maybe not attacked but yelled at or threatened a little—might have felt better than being ignored.

"No," Dawn said.

"We're all coming back next week," Dolores said, and no one disagreed.

Week 4

Halfway through their vigil a police car pulled up in front of them. Two officers, a man and a woman, climbed out. Jessie took deep, calming breaths and straightened to her full six-foot height, which gave her the slight satisfaction of looking down at them both. Dawn pulled her phone out. Beatrice, seventy-two and the oldest of them, said in a voice much wobblier and milder than her usual, "Have a blessed day, Officer! – Officers! What can we do for you?"

"You can move along and not block traffic, ma'am."

"Block traffic, Officer? Of course, we won't! I maybe did slow people down a little parallel parking—I'm not as fast as I used to be, I know—but I got my little van snugged right into the curb. She isn't blocking anybody now. And my goodness, Officers, we weren't going to walk out into traffic! I hate just trying to cross the streets here..."

"There's also foot traffic."

"Of course! So much better for the environment. Don't worry, we're not going to block up the sidewalk. We're just going to stand right here on the grass strip. Like that nice man down there with the hot dog cart." She gestured down the street to a hot dog cart. There was a substantial line in front of the cart, crowding the sidewalk. "Well, not quite like him. People don't show up for prayer the way they do for hot dogs. Sad, isn't it?"

"Have you been confronting people as they pass? Trying to make them stop and pray?"

"Oh no, that wouldn't do," Beatrice said.

"No, disturbing the peace wouldn't do," the female officer said.

"So that's why you're being nice to us?" Jessie asked.

The male officer laughed. "You have a good day, ladies. Come on, Allie, this lot isn't disturbing the peace. Or blocking traffic. We've got more important things to deal with. And you, ma'am, you take your time when you go to unpark that van. Take all the time you need." He was still chuckling as he and Allie got back into the cruiser and drove away.

Week 5

Three new people had traveled in the back of the church van. Five more had come in a car of their own from another town after seeing the clip of Beatrice's conversation with the police and sending her a message. Three other people who had walked past them repeatedly and slowed down enough to see their signs had also joined. They were getting somewhere, maybe.

Not far enough. It had been too easy to find eleven more faces for the THOSE WHO MOURN collection. Norma Cooper, dead when her dialysis was abruptly discontinued in the funding freeze. Isa Ghannam, disappeared from his college campus after a protest. Leila Smith-Abassi, killed by a US-built IDF-launched bomb as she tried to assist at a food distribution in a Gaza refugee camp...

The police car pulled up again. Well, *a* police car, with different officers, one taller than Jessie.

"Let's see your ID," said the tall one.

"No," Beatrice said, fishing the printout of the ACLU guide out of her purse and flipping through it. "We're not operating a motor vehicle. We don't have to show you ID."

"She does," the officer said, nodding toward Dolores.

"Racial profiling is illegal," Dawn snapped.

"Foreign nationals can be deported for anti-American behavior," the officer answered.

"Dolores is a citizen!" Beatrice countered.

"Shh," Ruth said. "Don't say anything except in the presence of a lawyer."

"That's for when you're getting arrested!" Dawn stage-whispered.

"Are you arresting me?" Dolores asked.

"We're asking you to come with us to clear some things up."

"Does she have a choice about that?' Ruth asked. "Dawn, are you recording?"

Dawn nodded.

"Let's see some ID," the officer said. "Or you can come along with me right now."

"Don't! What if they don't give it back?" Beatrice yelled.

Dawn knelt and began to sing in her fine soprano voice. Used to be called countertenor, back when Dawn had another name. Whatever anyone called it, it was cool and strong and true. "Were you there when they crucified my Lord?" she sang.

Jessie knelt, adding her hoarse contralto. The rest of the group joined in.

"There's no need for this," the officer said. "If you just..."

"Oh, sometimes it causes me to tremble, tremble, tremble!" the women sang, almost in harmony.

The officers hesitated, got back into their car, and drove away.

Jessie, rising heavily, saw a dozen people or so gathered around them.

"You OK?" asked a gray-haired man.

"Yes," Jessie said.

"But a whole lot of people aren't," Dolores added. "And we're here for them."

Those conversations took a while. They were still packing up when the representative's staffers came out of the building. One hurried across the street toward them. He looked to be about forty-odd like Jessie, sandy-haired and square-built.

"What can we do for you?" Jessie asked.

"He's supposed to be doing something for us," Dawn said.

"You think it's all about you, don't you?" the man said.

"I don't think you know me. I'm Beatrice. You're..."

"Richard Anderson. Not that you'd care. You all act like you're some kind of martyrs if the police ask you a simple question! And these signs! You'll carry on about all these media special cases. But do any of you care about normal Americans?"

"The Enriquez kids came to my day care until their dad got disappeared," Dolores said.

"Who are you calling abnormal?" Dawn demanded.

"Where were the signs and the singing when my

brother died?" Richard asked.

Dolores broke the ensuing silence softly. "I'm so sorry for your loss. What happened to your brother?"

"Forget it," he muttered.

"No," Dolores said, "we're here to remember. What happened to your brother? What was his name?"

"Dave. He wasn't stupid, whatever people like you think. He just... He hated to give up. He thought he could keep Dad's farm going. Tried to improve the herd, joined this new co-op for selling milk. Married, had the kids. Then... It wasn't a big farm, the kind the banks don't dare to drop. And he wasn't some fancy DEI person. Just a normal white American Christian guy with all that privilege we're supposed to have. So there weren't any special programs to help when the seed prices and the gas prices kept going up and the milk prices tanked, and he couldn't pay off his equipment loan. He had to let his helpers go, tried to do it all himself. Him and Marvin, when Marvin was out of school, but he always made Marvin do his homework, too."

"Marvin was his son?" Jessie asked.

"Yes. He was twelve. A growing boy. Dave made sure he got enough sleep. But Dave was out working eighteen, nineteen hours a day. He said it was his fault when the tractor rolled over on him, said he'd been stupid. Said the same thing last year when we found out he hadn't been able to stop taking the stuff they gave him for the pain when his prescription ran out." Richard's breath came hard and short. "We wanted him to go to rehab. He said he couldn't leave. Not then, not at haying time. I thought... He promised, in another month..."

"He didn't make it another month?" Dolores asked.

Richard turned away.

"I'm so sorry," Jessie said.

Richard turned back. "Mm-hmm. You liberals. I've seen the things you post about the kind of people who support Trump—rubes, stupid inbred people with bad teeth and dirty clothes who never went to college, meth heads. Dumb bigots who don't deserve anything. While we were mourning Dave, you know how many memes like that I saw from the guys I went to college with, guys who were all worked up about the election? Who hated President Trump just because he said people like my brother needed protecting?"

Several women answered. "That isn't why..." "But he isn't protecting anyone!" "You think Black farmers get better help?" And, in more than one voice, "I'm so sorry..." But Richard was already walking away.

Week 6

Richard answered the representative's phone on the third ring. Jessie knew his voice.

"Hello, Richard... Mr. Anderson. This is Jessie. From the prayer vigil."

"Yes?"

"I... Do you have a picture of your brother? Of Dave, who..." Was she just going to say *Your brother who died* to some near-stranger on the phone?

"You want me to prove he existed?"

"No! You said no one made signs when he died. I thought we could."

"Are you trying to lose me my job, too?"

"No!"

The call dropped.

That week, thirty-odd new people showed up at the vigil. Dolores and Beatrice handed out signs. Jessie noticed a young woman with a cross necklace and a microphone watching from the sidelines. The young woman caught her eye, waved, and came over.

"Have you come to join us?" Jessie asked.

The young woman gestured to a man with a video camera, who aimed it at Jessie, who wondered if she had brushed her hair that morning and also wondered why the cameraman was kneeling and aiming the camera up instead of standing and filming on the level. "We've come to cover the story," the young woman said. "I'm with a Christian women's blog. Our readers would love to know more about what you're doing here."

"Okay," Jessie said. "You probably want to talk to Dolores. She started this. Uh, I'm Jessie. You're..."

"Sybille. Jessie? Is that your full first name?"

"Jessica, but I like Jessie better. Now, this group..."

"This is a Christian women's group?"

"Well, it started with the women's Bible study," Jessie said, "but you can see some other people decided to join, too."

"But you were part of the original group? The women's Bible study?"

"Yes, and when Dolores suggested this, we were studying...

"How long have you been part of the *women's* Bible study?" Jessie bit her lip and hoped she was misunderstanding Sybille's emphasis.

"Since I moved into town."

Sybille held up her phone, showing one of the pictures from their church's website—the front door, the battered wooden steps, Beatrice's tulips, and the flag with its rainbow and triangle. "Is this your church?"

"Yes."

"That flag belongs to the church?"

"Sure."

"Is that why you went to that church?"

"Well..."

"Because it's a church that lets men go to the women's Bible study? And maybe other places as well?"

Jessie could feel her face and neck heating up. There were too many things she wanted to say at once, and none of them came out. She could say, truly enough, that she wasn't trans, but then it might sound as though she thought being trans was a bad thing, as though Dawn, who was shorter and curvier than Jessie but had been called a boy when she was born, was something less than a woman ...

"Which bathroom do you use in your church?" Sybille asked.

"We just have one. Unless you count the one in the basement that nobody uses because of the mold."

"Does your church believe God's truth about men

and women?"

"That in Christ there is neither male nor female?" Jessie mentally awarded a point to herself.

"So you don't have a problem with men lying about their identity so that they can prey on women?"

The heat in Jessie's face and neck spread to the rest of her. She wished she had the body Sybille apparently imagined her having—one that didn't get hot flashes when the brain that went with it was angry.

"Would you just shut up?" she growled at the bottom of her vocal range. "Would you just take your nasty little imagination and..."

Sybille beamed and turned away, the cameraman close behind her.

Jessie shoved her sign at Dawn and walked away. She walked a long time before the pounding heat in her body and her brain faded. When she returned most of the protestors had gone, but the church van was waiting for her.

As they loaded it, the representative's staffers scuttled back out. Dolores called, "Hello, Richard. How's Marvin?"

He didn't answer.

Week 7

Jessie watched the video clip a few dozen times. The low camera angle emphasized Sybille's soft curves, the height gap between Sybille and Jessie, and the hard angle of Jessie's jaw. Most of their exchange—Sybille's goading questions, Jessie's Bible quote and disarming answers—wasn't shown. Only the part about the flag, Sybille's question about men preying on women, and Jessie's furious response. Jessie thought ruefully of what Ruth had said about Dawn being able to make anyone who messed with them look bad. But that was different, wasn't it? Because Jessie and her friends were in the right? Though Sybille might think she was in the right, too... Sybille described their encounter as "another example of so-called TOLERANCE—letting men in women's clothes bully real women and tell us to shut up." It had received many likes and shares.

At the next vigil, a crowd of people stood on the facing sidewalk holding American flags, Trump flags, and banners reading REAL CHRISTIANS PROTECT REAL AMERICANS and REAL CHRISTIANS PROTECT REAL WOMEN.

Jessie took three deep calming breaths. "I'll be back," she said.

"Don't walk off on us again!" Beatrice's voice was tight. "I was so worried about you last time..."

"I'm not going far," Jessie said, nodding across the street.

"Don't!" Dawn urged.

"I'm sorry I messed up last time, but..."

"I'm not saying don't mess up. I'm saying don't get yourself hurt."

Jessie considered the banner-bearers. Most were women; many looked older than her. "I don't think they'll hurt me," she said.

"I'll go with you," Dolores said. "But if you get mad, breathe before you talk."

The silver-haired woman holding the right-hand end of the REAL WOMEN banner clasped her rosary and flinched as Jessie approached.

"Hello, and God bless you," Jessie said.

"Have you come to try and silence us?"

"No, I came to say hello to my neighbors."

"Neighbors?"

"Look, I'm trying to follow the commandment about loving my neighbors. Especially the least of these and the ones outside the camp, right? And the people we're mourning for are outside the camp to the President and his people, but you seem like you're outside my camp, so... Anyway, I'm Jessie. Who are you?"

"Why do you want to know?"

"It seems friendlier to call people by their names."

"Friendlier! Is it friendly to let men into the only safe places women have? Is it friendly to have men following women into their bathrooms and..." The older woman's voice roughened, stopped.

Jessie felt the heat surging in her again, along with the memories. All the times she'd been told she wasn't really a woman because she was too big, too square, too outspoken. Told, and...

The woman with the rosary was clearly remembering something, too. Something that hurt. Jessie had seen that look before.

"I'm sorry if you were... hurt by men, by a man—you, or someone you cared about," Jessie said. "I... haven't been hurt... that way. Maybe being big and getting mistaken for a man helped me out there, though it's also gotten me yelled at, and hit once or twice, by people who thought I wasn't the right sort of woman. But... I have family, friends—cis and trans—who've gotten... sexually harassed, or... assaulted. And I was so angry, and I felt so helpless. And..." She gestured toward the Trump flags. "When a man who'd boasted about groping women got elected.... that was so hard for some of them. And for me."

"That's a lie," a younger woman said. "They lie all the time about our President, when he's just trying to protect real Americans."

"From what?" Dolores asked.

Several people answered at once. "Aliens." "Terrorists." "Child traffickers." Dolores locked eyes with the woman who said in thickly accented English, "Communism."

"Communism?"

"Yes! I know what that does! I came from Poland, after..." The words seemed to choke her. "I lived under the Communists. I lived—I was lucky. But I know what they do."

"I am sorry," Dolores said. "It is so hard, to have to leave home because... because it has become terrible. My sister and I, we came that way, from Salvador. We came across the mountains and across the desert and we could have died, but we would have died from not leaving. Still, I miss hearing my own language all around me, and I miss my mother, and I miss the colors and the smells of what was my home. But this is my home now, where my friends and my little sister and her children live, and if I had to leave, I would be homesick as well as in danger."

"So, you're an alien?" said a taller, younger woman with a Trump flag.

"A citizen," Dolores said. "A citizen who remembers another place."

The Polish woman looked down. Nodded fractionally.

"Over there," Dolores said, gesturing across the road, "we are mourning with those who mourn. We are remembering the dead and the disappeared and the displaced. I will remember you. And if you ever want to join us, or to be remembered on our signs, you are welcome."

As they turned to go, the Polish woman called, "You are wrong, but God bless you!"

From across the road, a new member of Jessie's group yelled, "What do you know about real Americans, you fucking Nazis?" Jessie winced.

Week 10

Jessie frowned at her computer screen. It was her turn to write something to the Those Who Mourn mailing list, now that they had a mailing list and a protest permit and a page with almost a thousand followers—almost as many as the Real Americans Protect group which faced them across the street every week. Police vans parked near the protestors now, and they weren't encouraging opposing protestors to cross the street. No surprise, given some of the things that were yelled across the road in both directions. That was part of what Jessie had to try again to stop through the mailing list, though she wanted to yell, too, when she thought about the letters their church had received.

First the letters were about Jessie. Then some eager beaver on the Internet dug up an article from the time when the church put the pride flag up, which quoted Dawn as the only trans member of their little congregation. They also found and shared the church directory, and Dawn got some very unpleasant letters.

Dawn and Jessie glared at the women with the PROTECT REAL WOMEN banner every week, though they managed not to yell at them. But every Friday afternoon, Dolores waved to the Polish woman, and once the Polish woman waved back.

They saw less of the representative's staffers, because their permit only allowed them to gather in front of the public park a block down the street. But twice Dolores had seen Richard, waved, and shouted, "How is Marvin?"

Jessie didn't know how to write about that without making the question seem a staged gesture. How was virtue signaling different from not hiding your light under a bushel? Maybe she could write about that...

Her phone rang. In a raw voice, Dawn asked, "Do you have a minute?"

"Did you get another nasty letter?"

"Three, and the library's talking about having me not work with kids anymore. They called me in this morning. Said it wasn't about me, but the publicity..."

"That's terrible!"

"That's not the problem now," Dawn said. "I thought it was the problem this morning, and I tried to call Dolores and talk to her about it—you know the head librarian's grandkids go to her daycare, and... I didn't get her. I kept trying. She didn't even take my call during the kids' naptime. So, I called the daycare number, not her number. And I got Eddie." Eddie was Ediberto, Dolores' US-born nephew, who worked the same days she did at the day care center. "He was crying, and he said... he said ICE came, they came in a van, and they arrested Dolores."

"But they can't. She's a citizen," Jessie said, even as she wondered why this surprised her after all the stories on the signs she'd carried.

"They said she'd lied on her citizenship papers."

"Lied how?"

"Eddie didn't know. He didn't know where they took her, either. He was so sorry, said he should have figured out how to stop them or at least make them tell him something, but the kids were all freaking out, and he was trying to calm them down, and he was scared, too..."

"We should be able to call ICE and find out..."

"I've been trying ever since I called Eddie."

The entire women's Bible study tried calling that day and the next day and the next. There were no answers.

Jessie called Richard at the office. It was like talking to a machine. No information. No indication that he cared. Not when she reasoned, not when she shouted, not when she sobbed.

The women commiserated, sniped at each other, tried to make plans. Several people suggested it might be safer for Dawn not to go to the next vigil. Dawn said it wasn't her own safety she was worried about. On the next vigil day, Dawn was one of seven people gripping identical signs bearing Dolores' face. Six of them stood in the park.

Jessie snuck off and marched her sign up to the representative's office alone, the sharp wind cold on her skin and the heat welling up inside her. She banged on the locked door. Spoke into the buzzer and had to admit she didn't have an appointment (she'd been refused one). They didn't let her in. She stumped around the building and shook her sign at every ground-floor window.

An armed security guard who looked about seventeen approached her, looking nervous. "You come with me, ma'am," he said.

"Come where?"

"Like, in there." He gestured at the door she had banged on. "Um, and, ma'am, put your sign and your bag down, and keep your hands where I can see them."

She snorted, then bit her tongue, breathed deeply and followed the kid into the building, noticing gratefully that Dawn now stood out front filming her entrance.

The guard showed her into a little dim windowless room. *Interrogation chamber*, her brain whimpered. That was stupid, that was sensational. But she'd been imagining stupid sensational things ever since Dolores had vanished. Maybe that was why she'd come to the office: because she was tired of being the safe, protected, "real" American woman and wanted to try being the one in danger. But if that had been her wish, she now hoped fervently she wouldn't get it.

The boy went out and closed the door behind him. She heard the lock click.

As her eyes adjusted, she guessed that she was in a janitor's closet. Still, she was having some bad thoughts about the drain in the floor.

A few minutes later, Richard came into the room alone. Jessie flinched and set her back against a shelf of cleaning products. She'd opened the top of a jug of bleach which she figured she could throw at anyone who attacked her.

"You're afraid of me?" He sounded surprised. Sounded hurt.

"Why shouldn't I be?" she spat. "When you've had Dolores disappear and now, I'm locked in here—"

Richard raised his voice, cutting her off. "Don't make it all about you! Stop trespassing and interrupting government work. And answer your phone." He shoved something at her. A flip phone. Not hers. "Take it!" He was almost shouting now. "My advice, I mean. Take it, and... respond."

Jessie removed her hand from the bleach jug on the

shelf and took hold of the phone instead.

"Now, get out of here," he said, "and don't let me see you here again, or I'll call the police."

Jessie let herself be marched out the door, let the kid return her bag and sign to her. She hurried back to the park porta-potty, brushing off Dawn's questions and insisting that she had to pee immediately. She closed the door behind her before opening the phone.

She had one text message. It said, *Call me, Jessie James.*

There was exactly one person who called Jessie that.

Dolores answered on the fifth ring. "Good," she said.

"Where are you? Did they hurt you? Are you locked up?"

"I am not much hurt, and I was locked up and then put in a car, and I thought it was for deportation, but the car stopped in the middle of the night in the middle of nowhere, and the driver gave me this phone and told me to get lost. I am... I think it is better for me to stay lost, now, and there are people helping me do that. But I'm glad you got this phone. Give it to Eddie. He'll be half crazy worrying, that boy."

"You... you're okay?"

Dolores sighed. "Except for having lost my job and my home and being frightened and homesick and having to hide, yes, I am perfectly fine."

"How did you and Richard..." Jessie began.

"Are you talking in a safe place?"

"Maybe."

"Then least said, soonest sewn, yes?"

That had been a mistake, once, when Dolores was still feeling her way into English, but for years it had been a joke—and now, Jessie supposed, it was another clear sign that this really was Dolores talking to her. "This only, now," Dolores continued, all business. "Marvin and his mother had their food stamps cut. That's what the man who gave you the phone said. And I had kept asking about Marvin, I had cared, so when I was taken away, the man who gave you this cared about me, and he... he helped, as he could. And now I have to be quiet for a while."

The call dropped.

Jessie trudged back out to Dawn. "I'm okay," she said. "Talk later. Let's go back to the others before they all decide I've been sent to Siberia."

"Siberia? How did you know?" Dawn asked.

"Know what?"

"That Agata was with us and worrying about that sort of thing."

"Who?"

Dawn pointed to the Those Who Mourn line.

There were still six people holding up signs that showed Dolores' face. One of them was the Polish woman from the other side.

Hand-me-down

by Julia Figliotti

The sweater I'm wearing belonged to a
Sympathizer

The kind who sits comfortably
where evil meets idiocy
and drinks up what he's fed through
tubes painted red like the doors of those they tell us are
better off dead

And he feels no shame
only righteousness
in turning his back on the truth of his faith
like he's got no place in this fight for us

And he calls it sight—he says
that he sees through the bullshit and outside the lies

But then

How can you see through something sown deep within you?
Not just under your skin but inside your bones, too
seeping into your organs, heart beating a cruel tune
the oxygen carting rich poisons on trade routes
cleared by the medicine you won't deign to give thanks to
because you know better
and you refuse to be a debtor to a system that would center
humanity first, and knowledge, and giving up never

You don't need that shit, so you get rid of it
like it's just an old sweater

Letters of Hope

by A.M. Pennyfeather

My Darling Daughter,

My sincerest hope is that this letter finds you well.

Well...my sincerest hope is that you never see this letter, because if you're reading it, that means the protest today didn't end well for me. But if you are reading this...and I am gone...then I hope you are well.

I want you to understand why I'm doing this. Why I'm gone.

The best thing in my life right now is you. You're only three years old, and already the best person I've ever known. So vibrant and sweet. Your life can be so wonderful—you can be so wonderful—if you're given the chance.

But things right now are not good. You can't understand it at only three, but I pray that if you're reading this, you do.

The current regime will squash people like you.

People like the ones—the men—in charge right now will never respect such a strong, independent, unique young lady. They will never allow someone like you to exist freely.

That's why I'm going out this morning. There's a protest, you see. Those of us who are being pushed down are fighting back. The goal is peace, but we're not confident the other side will allow that. But that doesn't matter—we must stand! We can't let them win over and over until we have no freedoms left.

Until you have no freedoms left.

For the record: your father would be out there with me, but someone needs to take care of you. We went back and forth about who it should be, but it's my voice that this cry needs, so he's staying home with you.

I will go and I will fight! For you.

I want to see you grow up into the amazing person I know you will be. I want to watch as you learn, as you love, as you experience the beauty of this world! I want to take you to the beach—one of my favorite places as a child—so you can play in clean sand and splash in the perfect waves. I want you to experience the wondrous diversity of this world where people of all colors and orientations can unite, the way your father and I have. I want you to experience human art and how people can meld it with the beauty of nature to create its own kind of wonder.

But more important than watching you do these things is giving you the chance to do so. Or, at least trying to.

I can never apologize enough for not being there as you grow. I just pray this works. And that maybe you understand.

NEVER let them silence your voice. NEVER let them push you down.

And never forget that your mommy loves you—with every fiber of her being.

A tear dripped onto the wrinkled paper, as one has many times before. I dabbed at it with a tissue, careful not to smudge the ink. It was at that moment that my dad walked in.

"Sweetheart, they're ready for..." My dad slowed. A soft smile graced his full lips, and the familiar ghost of sorrow entered his eyes. "Reading your mom's letter again?"

I nodded and tried to stop more tears from doing further damage to my makeup. "I wish she could be here."

"I know." My dad took my arm and pressed his forehead against my temple. "But this is why she left that morning. And she would be so happy for you. And so proud of the incredible woman you've become."

I nodded again, but my throat was too full of emotion to form words. We stayed like that for several moments, until I could finally speak. "We should go. I don't want to keep everyone waiting."

"You're the bride. I don't think anyone will fuss at

you." My dad chuckled.

I laughed with him. "Well, if nothing else, I don't want to keep the other bride waiting."

My dad smiled and nodded, then waited patiently while I tucked my mom's folded letter into the long sleeve of my pink and orange gown. Then he took my arm and walked me out of the cabana and down the white aisle runner, held in place by painted stones at regular intervals. We paused at a flowery archway and waited for the acoustic guitar to play our march.

My dad and I stepped onto the soft white sand with the crashing waves keeping the beat for the musician. But I barely noticed any of this.

What held my complete attention was the woman in pink and blue walking toward me, her parents on either side. Her smile shined brighter than the sun, and her eyes sparkled more beautifully than the clear ocean when they met mine.

My pulse jumped, as it always did when I saw her, and the corner of my mom's letter scratched at my wrist.

It worked, Mom. Your sacrifice wasn't for nothing. Thank you.

A gentle breeze kissed my cheek as I took the hand of my beloved, and we turned to face the officiant and step into our future together.

The future that was fought for. That was won. And that I will never stop being grateful for.

Disunited States

by Brian U. Garrison

The government runs on volunteers.
The government is us.
The government was trying to tell us all along.
The government didn't always get it right, "We the people" left out quite a lot of people.
The government spent hundreds of years working to correct this oversight.

The government spent hundreds of years denying that it ever misspoke.
The government has half a mind still saying that not all people are people.
The government contains the capacity to care for all 300 million+ constituent elements.
The government lives with billions of symbionts.
The government exhibits several autoimmune quirks.

The government grows heads faster than the Hydra.
The government doesn't need to understand itself,
but it does need to stop eating itself alive.
The government requires collaboration to walk
forward.
The government runs on volunteers.
The government is us.

Midnight at the Barricades

by Christopher Scott Thompson

I was never able to remember, afterward,
Which sound had come first:
The rattling from my phone
As my ex-girlfriend Misty texted me,
Or the sound of the gunshots
From around the corner.

I'd been standing in front
Of one of the barricades
In the autonomous zone,
Staring out into the city at night.
I'd heard the rattle
Of the phone as the text came in,
And then a series of five shots...
Two, then a short pause, then another three.

Or else I heard the shots first
And then the phone.
I couldn't remember for sure,
And for some reason that bothered me.
If you can't count on time anymore,
What can you count on?

Anyway, I knew it was gunfire
Because it made a popping sound,
Unlike the loud bang of a firecracker.
The sound came from beyond the barricades,
But not far beyond.
Down by the cemetery of
Cardboard tombstones
Covered in the names of
People murdered by the cops.

A volunteer
Had been shot down there
A few nights before.
He had stepped outside the zone
And started walking
Down toward the cemetery
Where he'd parked his car,
And three shapes had
Stepped out of the darkness
And put a bullet in his gut.

He was not the only person

To get a gun pulled on him down here.
A friend of mine
Had been forced to lie down
On the street face-first
And robbed at gunpoint
Less than a block away.

Another night,
Some men in a van
Had tried to grab a teenage girl
A few blocks outside the zone
Before we came down
From the barricades
And ran them off,
Not knowing if they
Would open fire on us or not.

Some nights it was quieter.
Standing around and talking, mostly.
Opening the barricades
When a car came through
If it was someone who lived here.
But most nights, you heard gunfire.

A comrade
Unclipped his walkie-talkie
And held it up to his mouth,
Pressed the red plastic button.
"This is Station 1.
Five shots down by the cemetery, over."

There was a long, silent pause.
It was early autumn,
When the air is hot and thick
Even late at night.
A breeze blew down the street.
An empty paper cup
Came rattling along,
Skittered over to the nearby sidewalk.
One of the locals picked it up.

The walkie-talkie crackled
As a reply came through.
"Copy that.
Can you send us a few guys
For a minute?
We've got some out-of-town folks
Asking for an escort back to their car."

"Copy that. We're on the way."
I fell in beside him silently
As he adjusted the straps
On his plate carrier system.
I was the only one with no form of armor.
I was well aware
That we could be shot and killed,
That my comrades
Weren't wearing plate carriers
For their own amusement,
But I didn't have anything.

I couldn't afford anything.
None of the people
Who lived in the autonomous zone
Wore body armor anyway.
Only some of us volunteers.

Denny glanced in my direction.
"I can do this one, man. You don't have plates."
I only shrugged.
Denny looked away awkwardly.
There was nothing more to say.
It wasn't up to him to stop me
If I insisted on dying casually.

The women who wanted an escort
To their car were standing by the Memorial,
A place they'd driven
For several hours to come and see.
It was midnight, or close to it.
The third month of the Uprising.

The police had murdered a man
Just a few feet away.
Knelt on his neck
Till he stopped breathing,
Listening to him beg for mercy
The whole time as they killed him.
The city had burned
Because of that.

Images of the past three months
Played in front of my mind:
Sitting on a balcony
With an ancient rifle,
Guarding a synagogue
In case the Nazis came,
The bitter bite of smoke
On the nighttime air.

Escorting a journalist
Who needed bodyguarding,
Stinging clouds of teargas
In the downtown streets,
Unable to run fast
On my aging legs,
Hiding from soldiers
Behind a red brick wall
While white light
Bathed the night in front of us
As we waited for rescue.

Crouching with my head down
Behind one of these barricades
As voices crackled over
Our handheld radios:
"They're coming. They're coming!
Get your heads down!"

A bike messenger
With medical supplies

Who'd been shot at twice,
But who told the story
With a grin on their face.
Or perhaps that
Was the grimace
Of slowly fading fear.

A guy who passed
Around a bottle of whiskey
While we waited to get shot.
Covid? What Covid?
We're all about to die
Anyway, aren't we?

What was I
Doing out here,
After all?
I was a grown man, a father.
An anarchist, yes, but
What was I doing here?

Jim looked up and down the street,
Scanning from left to right.
No sign of any human being,
Just a stray cat that sat there
Staring at us
From on top of a recycling bin,
Maybe wondering
The same thing:

What are they doing out here, after all?

We stepped out
From behind the barricade
And walked up the street
To their waiting car,
Our eyes scanning the street the whole time.
“This is us right here,”
Said one of the women,
And we wished them
A good night before they drove away
Through the streets of a city
Of boarded-up windows,
A city where a thousand buildings had burned,
A city that had fought back
Against the idea
That the cops could just kill a man
And no one would do anything about it.

Now there were no cops
On the streets of this city
But that didn’t mean
The killing had stopped.
People were shooting
Each other
Every single day.
That’s just the kind of country
We live in, I think.
The kind of country
We’ve built.

We were almost back to Station 2
When I heard a pop,
Realized someone was shooting
From behind us,
And started to run.

The three of us
Dove down
Below the barricade at Station 2.
The gun popped again,
But from this distance
It sounded much louder.
Three shots came in,
Followed quickly
By the sound of another weapon.
This one almost barked,
One angry shot after another.
A third gun followed suit.

The zone was under attack
By at least three armed men.
"Jesus," one of my comrades said,
Although he was not a religious man.
Getting shot at repeatedly,
Well, it tends to bring that out.

Some guys
Came running down the street
From inside the zone,

Pulling their own pieces as they came in.
What else could they do?
If you're getting shot at,
It's only reasonable to return the favor.
As we crouched down
Behind the barricade
And did our best not to die,
They raised their guns
And sent their bullets
Into the night.

I was hiding
Behind a concrete barrier
As two gangs of young men
Waged a gunfight
With each other right over my head.
And what did I feel?
I felt nothing.
Not fear
Not anger
Not anything at all.

But if I wasn't feeling,
I was thinking.
I was thinking about
The mountain.
A mountain of cans and boxes,
Rice and beans.
A pyramid of groceries
In the middle of the street

That anybody could take from
Without paying anything.

And I was thinking about the sign
Up near the barricade:
"No violence, and no for-profit sales."

No violence? Well, okay.
It wasn't working out like that.
In a country like this one
That was maybe a bit much.
But a place that
Said no to profit?
A place where no one was hungry?

Where no one had to count pennies
To buy a packet of Ramen noodles
Or make a choice between
Rent and groceries...
Can you imagine a place like that?
Can you imagine fighting for it?

Yeah, that's something I'll fight for.
And then there's the guy
In the neighborhood
Who told me
He had never known anyone,
Never talked to anyone here,
Until the barricades went up.
Now he talks with people

All the time.
Borrowed a cup of sugar
From a neighbor just the other day.
Sits outside on the street corner
All night, just passing the time
With his new friends.

When I walked around
Those streets,
Past the little homemade library
And the gas station
They'd changed into
The People's Way,
I saw a place
Where people were building something
That doesn't exist in this country.
Something human beings need.

And yeah, that's something I'll fight for.
So that's why I was here,
Crouching down behind a concrete wall
While the young men
Shot at each other.

There weren't any bodies.
Most people don't know this,
But it's usually like that.
Shooting at other people
Who are shooting at you
Is not so easy.

"You alright?" I asked
My comrade Denny
A few minutes later
As we turned the corner
And walked down the street
Toward Station 1.

Denny only shrugged.
"It's just another fucking Monday."
He glanced at my face.
"Didn't you have a text?"

I pulled out my phone,
Saw that the message
Was from my ex-girlfriend Misty.

Are you okay out there? I'm worried...

I grinned in silence.
Nine months ago,
Before the plague came,
We'd been walking
Through the streets of this city
Hand in hand.
Telling each other we loved each other,
Making empty promises
About a forever that was never going to happen.

Now the city had burned.

All the shops
Were boarded up,
Empty faces with their eyes blank,
Staring out at the city in horror.
Together, we'd fought back, yes...
But we were paying for it.
And who knew how much more
We would have to pay?

Gunmen roamed
The streets of the city at night.
And I was out here with them,
An unarmed man in a war zone.

Yes, I had wanted her.
I had wanted a different future than this.
But my life was different now,
And what did that dream
Have to do with it?

I had found a new dream here,
And it wasn't just for me.
A dream of a better world
That at least seemed possible.

I Saw a Woman in Chains Today

by Trixie Belka

I saw a Woman in Chains today
the first time I saw her, I assumed she was resting
Heavy-set, my age, off her feet, glaring up at us passing from under her eyebrows
or maybe the glare was my post-interpretation
her two companions were standing on the other side of the very narrow hallway within arm's reach of her
I had to turn sideways to get past them
they all made me feel very small not short but actually small
I AM NOT SMALL i am short
it wasn't until the doctor muttered Corrections Department as we came back to the lobby
that I glanced down at the
heavy-set
Middle-aged

woman of color
sitting off her feet
I only then saw that there was a chain, like a heavy dog leash, stretched across her body
Under her ample bosom (no, not staring at her bright green-shirted chest, was that why I'd missed it before?)
Lashing her arms down to her sides,
and she was not sitting there to rest, not her choice
Looking up without meeting anyone's eyes, but does that make it a glare?
I had never seen a woman in chains before
Outside of Red Sonja,
And some crazy friends at a punk concert a long time ago in a cold land far away
I don't watch that stuff online
And those ink sketches of suffering African or Indigenous women in history books were always distorted and unreal cartoons
Never like this
In a suburban medical office
Pressed up between the air conditioner and a red medical waste bin
I hope if I ever see that again
it is because that woman has chosen chains and is enjoying it in some consensual situation or cosplay
This woman, like so many of her ancestors, was not.
And all I did, my fine feminist short self, was bear witness and be disturbed.
It's never enough.

A White House

by Anonymous

You inherited it from your grandparents. The home has been in your family for multiple generations—the kind of place that many have lived in, but no one has moved out of.

The day you get the keys, you're confronted by sights both familiar and strange. The record player in the corner was the soundtrack to your childhood. The cast iron skillet serving up daily fried eggs. Black and white vintage tiles in the bathroom.

But also, mold around the tub—a lurid halo your grandparents never would have stood for decades ago when they had their health. Expired food in pantry shelves. A box of never-installed door stops. A dusty walker and hospital bed in the main bedroom.

With a few months' elbow grease, you can restore this place to its former glory. Maybe even give it the update it's been needing for years.

You recognize just how fortunate you are to own a home at all. Even if it came at the cost of losing the grandparents who raised you.

So, you dedicate your evenings and weekends to cleaning. Bulky trash pickup becomes your friend. You buy gallons of fresh paint from the hardware store, and you start planning a yard sale.

All is going well, until it isn't.

The central wooden beam in the living room ceiling cracks ominously. You hurry from the kitchen to see a jagged seam that wasn't there before. You grab some 2x4s from the garage and wedge them between the beam and the floor.

Two days later, you take a few hours off work to meet a structural engineer at the house.

"Oh yeah. That's a problem."

"Is the ceiling going to collapse?"

"Might could." He puts on his ballcap. "Lemme guess, you've got an attic full of stuff."

It honestly never occurred to you to check. You pull a cord to reveal a foldable ladder and climb up. You're greeted by a cavern of boxes and cobwebs, stacked high to the rafters. You pull the light's cord and shift out of the way so the engineer can see.

"There's your problem. No more than twenty pounds per square foot up here, alright?"

It's a veritable dam of family heirlooms. It's impossible to know how long it will take to sort through. "How much time do I have?"

"The weight isn't going away on its own, and the structural integrity of the house is already compromised. So, you tell me, how much do you want your ceiling to stay up?"

So, you set the sponges and paintbrushes aside and start working on the new project. The entrance to the attic is twenty feet from the broken beam, but you'll have to unearth your way to it inch by inch, like an archaeologist with a trowel.

After the engineer leaves, you grab the first box and carry it downstairs. Another, another, another.

You work into the evening before rewarding your curiosity about the contents. Under a lid is a grade school photo of you, missing a front tooth, hair imperfectly combed. Underneath are reams of assignments, report cards, and graduation announcements. You touch the embossed letters and smile. You weren't the best student, so it's touching your grandparents kept so much. The memory of their congratulatory hugs that day are bright—the feeling of your grandfather's scratchy beard against your ear, the way your grandmother fussed over your robe and cap. There, at the bottom of the box, is your tassel.

Most of this could be digitized, so you start a pile at the head of the dining table, where your grandfather used to eat.

Over the next few days, you come away with taxes to shred, a dry-rotting doll that belonged to your aunt, and chintz couch cushions long out of fashion.

It's not until the following weekend that you find it: a box with a historic deed to a home a state away, deeper in the South. For a moment, you wonder if the property is still in the family, but then you find a bill of sale, a hundred years old. When you look up the location, the house is gone, but the land is still dotted with former slave cabins—turned into vacation rentals. Your stomach turns.

Under that paperwork is a circular patch featuring a white cross on a black background. You've seen this emblem before in history books.

Ugh, god. Why the hell is this in your house?

You dub it "the box of racist shit," and you shove it back upstairs into the attic. You should burn it, right? There's no place for any of that in today's world.

But maybe a museum would be interested? Or an archive?

It's a problem for another day when you have the energy to confront it.

In the short term, you've redistributed the weight in the attic and begun working in earnest on the yard sale coming up in just a week.

The more anonymous the item, the easier it will be to sell. The toy chipmunk in the shiny tin pail. The vintage dresses. The piles of cookbooks.

You dedicate your evenings to writing signs, pricing items, and searching for folding tables.

The day of the yard sale arrives warm and bright. You set up the heirlooms and check the small bills in your pocket. The shoppers arrive before you're technically open, but you welcome them. They'll give these items new life, new stories.

A boy and his dad beam as they buy a couple of fishing poles. A young woman sways in a silent, solo dance as she holds up a checkered skirt to her waist. A couple eagerly takes your grandmother's sewing machine off your hands.

It all changes at noon.

Crrrrrr—BOOM!

Windows shatter, and the roof sags.

You run to the front door, but you can't push it open with all the debris behind it.

A neighbor, who had stopped by to shop, hurries to help you. "Holy!"

Your voice is weak. "The engineer warned me there was too much in the attic?"

"Can I help?"

No, of course not. You were raised to resist help. But who said? Your grandmother? A thousand generations of deferential Southerners and Englishmen before them.

"Maybe we can push the door open."

"Of course."

You brace, pushing.

Something shatters at the force, and the door gives, tilting inside with a screech of protest.

You both see it at the same time. The box with the white hood and cross has spilled its contents on top of everything else from the attic.

You scramble to block your neighbor's view, but it's too late.

They back out of the door hurriedly, eyes wide.

"I promise, it's not mine. I just—"

"I gotta go."

You feel hollow as they speed walk down the driveway.

The yard sale shoppers trickle away, and you are

alone.

But if you had made a different choice... if you had steeled yourself after seeing what the darkest recesses of the attic contained... would it have made a difference?

The ceiling has not yet collapsed. Dust is in your hair. Boxes surround you.

And in front of you is clear evidence of the horrifying history of your family.

Why didn't your grandparents dispose of this? Why did they leave it here to molder among the mundane artifacts of life?

They're just things. But some things carry so much meaning, so much weight. So much toxicity, hatred, and pain.

You owe it to yourself to confront it all.

You bring down the box of racist shit.

Work on the attic stops as you dig deeper, finding evidence the cloak and hood belonged to your great uncle. The plantation owner was his great-grandfather.

Only five generations ago. That's not a long time.

Should you take on the blame?

You enslaved no one. You subjugated no one. You feel, in your heart of hearts, you've personally done nothing wrong. And that means there's no cause to be ashamed of who you are, of the white-skinned body you were born into.

And at the same time, it's clearer than ever that you have personally benefitted from a fundamentally racist system. That your family participated in it, perpetuated it.

Could you have inherited this home without a family

legacy of privilege and wealth made on the backs of enslaved people?

Their descendants—could they afford this?

There is no shame in who you are, you decide. But there is responsibility.

You cannot change the past, but you can take steps to make the present moment more equitable.

So, each night after work, you pull down a few more boxes to continue relieving the weight on your ceiling, and when your arms tire, you switch to research.

You find bills of sale of human beings. Dig into genealogy research. It's spotty. But you learn there is a local family who carry your same last name but not your skin color who, it's almost certain, are related to the souls who your not-so-great-great-great-grandfather enslaved. And from what you're finding, it's likely you're actually related by blood.

How does one reach out through the murk, through the shame?

But you find a way. You introduce yourself over email.

You let them know what you've discovered.

You apologize for the immense harm your family caused.

You let them know you just inherited this home. That you want to sell it. Start fresh with your own place.

And you'd like to give them half of the proceeds as reparations.

It doesn't fix what was done.

It doesn't erase generations of poverty and discrimination that followed their freedom.

But it feels right.

You go out for a meal. You and this stranger—this relative—connect. Over hobbies, over work, over books.

It's awkward.

It's hard.

It's worth doing.

They are immeasurably gracious. Unnecessarily so.

The third time you meet over burgers, they call you a friend.

You still have the yard sale.

The ceiling still collapses.

But you're no longer left alone.

The more the house sells for, the more everyone receives. So, your friend arrives to help. Together, you sell what contents can be salvaged. Together, you repair the roof. Together, you drink beers as you watch the hood and cloak burn in the backyard fire pit.

And when someone new buys the house, you keep just enough to buy a small place. The rest of it—the lion's share—is theirs. After all, their family earned it generations ago.

The Cycle

by Kurt Newton

When the violence of kings
brings a nation to war...
The cycle repeats,
we've been here before.
When the license to cheat
becomes too easy a chore...
The cycle repeats,
we've been here before.
When the widening gyre sings
of better days on some distant shore...
The cycle repeats,
we've been here before.
When the devils inside us
bristle and chide us...
When the angels beside us
can no longer guide us through the door...
The cycle repeats,

we've been here before.
When the youth fill the streets
in favor of justice ignored...
The cycle repeats,
we've been here before.
When the unfulfilled plead
for a savior to stand up and say, "NO MORE!"
The cycle repeats,
we've been here before.
When the brilliance of strangers
help the weak, the endangered...
When the resilience of hatred
fades like a stain on the Declaration
we agree we're all fighting for...
The cycle repeats,
we've been here before.
When the silence of peace
becomes a heavenly roar...
The cycle is complete,
we've been here before.

In the Shadow of the Last Blossom

by Stephanie Carrier-Boodram

I love basking in the sun. I believe it should be a duty for all living beings on this planet—a daily moment to savor, something to do every single day. When the sun's warm rays caress my fur, it feels as if everything else fades away, like a gentle warmth slowly spreading, soothing every fiber of my being. It's a feeling of calm, of regeneration, a moment when everything falls into place, as if the sun is nourishing both my thoughts and my soul. Nothing in this world compares to this pure moment of tranquility. That's why I am constantly in search of this little joy.

As summer comes to an end and the season of endless rain approaches, I must make the most of my outings to the park. The sun is most enjoyable there.

The morning sun is still a bit shy when I slip out of the house. My home—a dark, damp basement apartment—doesn't provide enough space for me to stretch my legs properly. My owner doesn't seem to understand that I don't like dark corners. She leaves me there alone, dozing off on a worn-out rug. But I know where to find the real sun.

I only must cross the street. My claws click against the sidewalk as I make my way to the park. I am already at the edge of the path, where the trees open to let the golden rays in. The afternoon sun is waiting for me right there, ready to warm me to the bone. I stretch, my supple muscles tightening, then roll in the grass, intoxicated by the fresh scent of earth and flowers. The sound of water trickling from the fountain soothes me.

Lying on my back, I watch the squirrels playing among the branches. A few pigeons are gathered around a trash can on the right-hand path. They look like they're deep in discussion, deciding what to have for dinner from their refrigerator.

Near a patch of multicolored flowers, a pair of dragonflies perform a fascinating courtship dance.

Truly, here, everyone is free to be whoever they want.

I'm thirsty. I stretch my back legs, then my front ones, and head toward the fountain. A little sip will surely be refreshing. Just as I start drinking, I feel eyes on me. Two small gray rats, perched on the edge, are watching me and whispering.

"Hey buddy, isn't this water just delicious?" One of them snickers.

I ignore his provocation and continue lapping up the cool water.

"Well, aren't you quiet, Your Majesty," disparages the other. "Is the water to your liking, or should we flavor it for a noble like yourself?"

I raise an eyebrow but don't respond. The rats burst into laughter and scurry away, chattering.

"Oh, look at him, all proud with his twitching whiskers. He still thinks the park belongs to him."

Ah, those rats! They think they can do whatever they want just because there are so many of them and they've survived every plague in history.

I hop down from the fountain and head toward the bench on the right-hand path, near the trash can where the pigeons are gathered. I feel like taking a nap. There's still some time before the sun starts to sink too low. But after I leap onto the bench, a sharp whistle startles me.

"Halt!" a shrill voice commands.

A plump brown rat, wearing a red belt adorned with a golden whistle, stands before me with crossed paws.

"This bench is now reserved exclusively for rats, and as far as I can see, you belong to a different species."

"What?" I protest. "Since when? Benches have always been for everyone!"

"Not anymore. This one is strictly for rats."

I turn back with a loud sigh, hoping to make my frustration clear, but he doesn't seem affected in the slightest.

Annoyance rises within me, and I suddenly have the urge to sharpen my claws to blow off some steam. That old oak tree over there will do just fine. But as soon as I extend my claws, another sharp whistle cuts through the air.

"Violation! You're damaging the park," the damn brown rat yells.

"What? It's a tree, not private property," I retort.

"Everything must be respected. You're defacing park property. I'll have to issue you a fine."

"What? I barely touched it! This isn't your tree or your park. It belongs to everyone."

At that moment, rats seem to appear from everywhere. Some glare at me with disdain, others whisper among themselves. A shiver runs down my spine. Since when do they have so much authority?

The pigeons, usually noisy, have fallen silent. The squirrels watch from afar, as if realizing—too late—that the park is no longer the one they once knew.

I look for an escape. I spot a stretch of flowers and move toward them, hoping to roll around and regain some of that freedom I love so much. But as soon as I set a paw on the petals, a third whistle pierces the air.

"No stepping on the flower beds!"

I freeze. I feel the weight of countless gazes pressing down on me. I should have acted sooner, when there was still time. But now, it's too late. Around me, freedom has vanished, and I find myself trapped in a park that is no longer mine...

The Playbook

by Benjamin Gorman

It's not just the silence
of good people.
It's the participation.

They go after the powerless first
but they also endeavor
to convince you
to help
spread the word
share the lie
tell a joke
throw a stone.

Protect the targets
but also pay attention
to the casual assistants.
Today's toadies
are tomorrow's foot soldiers
until they are the targets
asking you for protection.

Neon-Nazis

by Casey Aimer

I patrol my ship city's halls
for new neon-Nazi stickers.

My arms peel away sticky history,
erase their claims to these spaces.
They dress up old hatred in pretty
colors calling it new subterfuge,
twist words 'til terror is peace.

I replace each with whole-
some anti-fascist holo decals
declaring the sectors ours, as if
capturing corridors with markings.

Carefully, I leave plenty of evidence.

I hold an ID spoofer and practice mimicry,

confusing cops while framing neon-Nazis
for this invisible underground vandalism
war visible only to those caring enough
to persuade others through propaganda
towards love or malice via tiny stickers.

But I've scrambled IDs so long,
including mine, I barely know
what I call myself, or if I matter
when ideas and causes are staked.

When walking through my ship
often I forget I have no legs,
moving through cameras or
arms extending from ceilings.

On lucid ship nights I remember
I'm a subroutine, or the ship itself.

Corporate Baby

by J.L. Henker

Dr. Sandoval adjusted the collar of her white coat and scowled at her screen. Lights glistened off her blood-red lipstick and the corporate logo affixed to her starched collar. She frowned at the young woman in a business suit sitting on the other side of her desk. “Kirsen, you’re overdue for this procedure. Is there a problem?”

“No.” Kirsen shifted on the hard chair. “I’m overwhelmed with taking care of my mother’s estate.”

The doctor tapped the screen and paused. “My condolences. She was an important asset.”

A bitter taste rose in Kirsen’s mouth. Like many women chasing a decent job and stability, her mother signed a contract binding herself and future children to Locus International. She had been nothing more than a corporate asset and now, so was Kirsen. Bastards. She faked a smile. “Show me the candidates.”

The doctor swiveled the screen so Kirsen could view

bios of four men, their first names, job titles and asset numbers under their photographs. Her stomach soured.

"These are your best matches."

Biochemistry, astrophysics, physician, engineer. Kirsen ground her teeth. What about artists or musicians?

"If you can't decide, we can choose one for you," the doctor said, feigning helpfulness.

Kirsen stood and stepped toward the door. "You pick."

The doctor adjusted her computer screen and clicked open her appointment calendar. "When can you..."

"I'll check my schedule and get back to you." Perspiration broke out on Kirsen's forehead. Stalling was a risky move. The company evicted people from their corporate-owned apartments for less. An ex-colleague lived in abandoned city tunnels; there were also rumors of settlements in the far northern provinces. They believed surviving in harsh conditions away from city comforts was better than being a corporate lackey. Kirsten grimaced. *Am I that courageous?*

As she followed the sterile white hallway to the exit, she passed the Pediatric Research and Assessment waiting room. Children fidgeted in their seats, scared and subdued. Kirsen remembered the strange doctors, blood tests, brain scans... She shuddered. No. Not this way. Never.

Kirsen burst past the security guard and through the front doors. She marched several blocks to Locus Park and followed a gravel path to her favorite bench underneath an ancient maple tree. It was quiet this time of day—too early for after-work joggers and too late for nannies and babies. The sun arched overhead and created mottled shadows on her skin as she pondered her options.

A woman in a hooded sweatshirt appeared from behind a large azalea bush and walked toward her. The approaching figure lowered her hood and raised her hands. "Don't worry. I'm not from corporate."

Kirsen frowned. "What do you want?"

The woman plopped down and tugged her sleeve to expose a jagged scar. "I cut it out myself."

Kirsen grimaced. "How did you know..."

"We tracked your appointment data. Our hackers are pretty good."

Kirsen glanced around to make sure no one was close enough to overhear.

"Relax. The cameras don't cover this section of the trail. If you want our help, be at the corner of 14th and Bridgeton at 3:00 p.m. tomorrow. Someone will pick you up and take you to one of our centers. They'll use a blocker to prevent you from being tracked." She tapped her scar. "They'll do a much better job taking out yours."

"How do I..." Before Kirsen finished her sentence, the woman got up and hustled away.

A chill ran up her spine. Was this a trap—or an escape route?

Kirsen glanced at her phone. It was 3:15, and no one had arrived. She paced nervously and searched for an approaching vehicle. Daily news reports announced resisters being arrested for defying corporate policy. What if no one showed up? She took a deep breath and rubbed her hands. A battered BMW pulled alongside and a woman with gray hair and a wrinkled face rolled down the passenger window. "Kirsen?"

She nodded.

"Get in."

The woman drove erratically, taking random left and right turns. She stopped every few minutes to check her GPS and look over her shoulder. They rolled to a stop in front of a run-down, gray apartment building, and she pointed. "It's on the second floor. Apartment 213. Good luck."

Kirsen slid from the back seat and closed the door. As soon as it clicked shut, the car sped off. She turned toward the building and hesitated. Something was off. It was too quiet. A flash of gray appeared on the left side of the building as Corporate Police surged around the corner and clamored up the stairs she'd been about to ascend. She didn't wait to see where they were going. She already knew.

Kirsen threw her phone on the table. A blinking red display announced three new messages. Two were from the doctor's office. The last, sent moments before, was from Corporate Compliance. She was out of time.

She rummaged through her kitchen and filled a backpack with energy bars, water, transit passes, cash, and a heavy sweatshirt. Her phone rang again. They would come for her soon. She turned on her sound system, cranked up the volume, and collected a sharp paring knife from her kitchen.

She placed the knife on the edge of her bathroom sink and rummaged through a cabinet for a first aid kit and a bottle of alcohol. Her hands trembled as she poured it over the knife. *Took it out herself, she said. Oh god.* Pinching her wrist, she located the chip under several layers of skin. She pushed the knife tip into her flesh and under the tiny piece of metal. The pulsing music muffled her cry. She dug deeper, but the wires connected to the tracker anchored it in place, and it refused to budge. *Crap. I need tweezers.* She rifled through a drawer and found a pair at the bottom. She clasped the chip and pulled. It strained against the wires connected to her nerves and popped out. She stifled a scream and dropped to her knees. Tears streamed from her eyes. *Got you, you bastard.*

Blood poured from the wound and onto her bathroom rug. She washed the gash with hydrogen peroxide, wrapped her wrist tightly, and took a pain pill. The silver chip sat in a pool of blood in her sink. "Fuck you, fuck Corporate," she said, and flushed it down the toilet. She took one last glance around her apartment, grabbed her backpack, and opened the door. Checking to make sure the hallway was clear; she avoided the elevator and fled down the back stairs.

Three hours later, Kirsen hunched and shivered on the park bench where the underground network had found her the day before. Her wrist was on fire; the bandage was soaked in blood. She hissed in pain.

Crap, I'm probably in shock. What if no one comes? I'll probably end up unconscious in a hospital somewhere until Corporate identifies me.

A woman in a dark blue jogging suit emerged from the trees and ran toward her. She sat down and pointed to Kirsen's wrist. "Let me see."

She held up her arm.

She whistled between her teeth. "Not the worse DIY job I've seen, but you've lost too much blood." The woman clasped her elbow. "Can you stand?"

Kirsen took a deep breath and struggled to her feet.

The women nodded. "How's it feel being an outlaw?"

Kirsen was in too much pain to answer, but she raised her good arm and clenched her fist.

She placed their arm around Kirsen's waist and guided her toward a waiting car. A bearded man in a red ski cap jumped out and opened the side door. He saluted. "Welcome to the underground."

It Won't Happen Here, Not to Me

by Julia Figliotti

"I believed you," she says
Tears threatening to spill past the gate

Welling up in humiliation and betrayal, just shy of
Overflowing like a raging cataract pouring through
    crevices
Naturally formed over time as a
Trickle became a stream until current events turned
    it violent.

Harmonious celebrations of established foundations
All of a sudden screeching, discordant, as the
Preachers become ignored by the god they adore
Pathetic and grasping and mumbling their lasting
Excuses, how it was okay when the target was you

but
"Not like this," and "I'm not supposed to be on that list," and

"How was I supposed to know they'd come for me next?" when
Everyone said that would follow in step
Reality shows us again and again that none are exempt, not
Even you

Not when you voted for exactly this as you told us we were
Overreacting, crying our blizzard of snowflake
Tears born of storybook fears—not when you

Told us this was the best chance we had
Of achieving the freedoms we boast in "our" land and

Maybe you're finally starting to learn that those
Enterprising tables don't ever quite turn

The Day They Shot Khalil Rucker

by Madeline White

The end of everything started six days before they shot Khalil Rucker.

Before they put him between a wall and a firing squad, Khalil was four things. He was a good person. He was Bogden Fields' best friend. He was a hero. And he was a man who dropped a nuclear bomb on his own people.

Six days before they shot Khalil Rucker, he was called up by his commanding officer for a briefing. Khalil left his standard-issue chicken-fried steak in anonymous brown sludge, half eaten on his plastic tray and set off straight from the mess hall, stride sure and eyes star-spangled. He came back glazed and stumbling, with vomit on the collar of his fatigues.

"You've been selected for a top-secret mission," the

man with all the brass had said. "Tell no one."

Instead, Khalil told Bogden.

"It's a nuclear drop," he whispered through his cigarette smoke, leaning against the wall behind the mess hall. "Bombs the size of the ones they dropped on Hiroshima and Nagasaki. And there's twelve, just on my plane alone."

Bogden's guts wrenched into coils at this, and he regretted finishing Khalil's chicken-fried steak. "How many planes are there?"

A group of guys jogged by in sweat-soaked shirts and silkies, led by a man who looked like a German action figure. They were singing "Marine Boot Camp," their boots slamming the concrete in rhythm with the cadence.

"I'll make your life as miserable,
As miserable as I can,
And when you finally leave this place,
You'll be a fighting man."

The friends stopped talking and kept smoking until the group passed.

"I dunno," Khalil whispered when they were gone. "But I think it's a lot."

Khalil's dark skin looked vaguely green and Bogden was pale as hell, the horror almost too much for either of them to think about.

Bogden knew the war wasn't going *well*. He might be a jar-headed crayon-eater and a terminal Lance to boot, but you didn't need to ace your ASVABs or have yourself a shiny diploma to know that. He knew five years of war and more dead friends than he could count wasn't what the brass called a *favorable outcome*. But this... This was extreme. Really fuckin' extreme.

"You're sure they ain't dummy rounds or somethin'?" he asked Khalil, grasping at straws.

Luckily looks couldn't kill, because Khalil never missed. Bogden spat into the dust of the jogging path.

Then Bogden dropped his voice, not because there was anybody around, but because you never knew who might be listening. There weren't as many cameras and mics live on base as the brass wanted guys to think there were, but there were still more than you'd want. With most folks having mixed feelings about the war at best, it was always a good idea to know where they were, and then be careful in case you were wrong.

"What are you gonna do?" Bogden asked Khalil.

He didn't know what made him ask it. It was a dipshit question, because when you got an order, there was only one thing *to* do: follow it.

But he asked anyway, and instead of stating the obvious, Khalil put his cigarette to his lips for a long, long time, and when he finally he pulled it away, he said, "I don't know."

The end of everything actually started five years before they shot Khalil Rucker. There was a protest, a big one, that erupted all at once in New York, Washington,

D.C., San Francisco, Austin, and Atlanta–like a multi-headed hydra bursting from the surface of a restless sea.

It wasn't the first protest, or even the first to hit the whole country at once. Folks had been taking to the streets more and more often for years, over everything from foreign policy to civil rights to Presidential election results.

So, when the city blocks filled up with hundreds and thousands of old people, black masks stark against thinning grey hair, folks didn't immediately think a lot of it. When those old people started shouting about how they were tired of being forgotten–allowed to die of a string of viruses, then lack of healthcare, and the spluttering end of Social Security–people turned the channel to golf, or the Superbowl, or *Love in Prison* or whatever the fuck. People had gotten tired of protests somewhere in the 2040s, and by the time the old people flooded the streets, it took more than a few broken windows or megaphoned voices to catch the public's attention.

Then the bodies started to drop.

Not a few bodies, like when the police fired rubber bullets into crowds and called it "tragic" that some people's soft flesh couldn't meet hard projectiles point-blank and not crumple like wet paper onto the concrete. Not a reasonable amount of bodies for a "thoughts and prayers" sort of tragedy, like when gunfire broke out and nobody could tell you who started it. But a load of bodies. "Can't run without tripping over one" numbers of bodies. "Blood running into the gutters" numbers of bodies. "Every news channel turned to live coverage of the massacre" numbers of bodies.

It was a slaughter. Police in riot gear and soldiers in the National Guard versus grandmas with knit cozies on their molotovs. Grandfathers holding their canes in front of their wrinkled faces as if varnished wood could stop bullets.

In the days after, they called it the Grey Uprising.

In the days after, the streets burned.

Maybe, if you wanted to get philosophical with it, you could say that the end of everything started hundreds of years before they shot Khalil Rucker. Back when a bunch of rich white guys with ugly shoes and powdered wigs decided that it was legitimate and justified to wage a war in order to be freer, just so long as it was their freedom on the table. That it wasn't "destroying your own community" or "civil war" if you were the one who got to write the history books.

You could say that the end of everything was built into the foundation from those very first bricks, and you might be right. But at the very latest, the end started nine days before they shot Khalil Rucker, when a bunch of old commanders with too-tight uniforms and too many ribbons got together in Washington, D.C. It only took thirty-seven minutes of spirited discussion for them to conclude that it was legitimate and justified to drop a barrage of nuclear bombs on their own people. The line, it seemed, came when your "civil war" was about to become a brand new nation's "revolution."

"It's a small price to pay," somebody with a grey mustache probably told somebody else with a grey mustache, "for freedom."

Then the second grey mustache probably agreed, because how could you expect to have freedom if you weren't an American? If you seceded from the union, how was anyone supposed to make sure you got the life you deserved?

But the end of everything turned from words to a concrete wall behind Khalil's head the night after he got his orders, when he and Bogden stood on watch in front of the barracks at three in the morning and Khalil whispered to his friend that he couldn't do it.

From the same armpit small town in rural Virginia, Bogden and Khalil had enlisted together, when the mass recruitment push in the wake of the Grey Uprising had promised college, a housing fund, and a hefty retirement check for anyone who joined the fight against the would-be separatists. For two down-home boys itchin' to crawl out of the trailer park, politics weren't even part of the equation.

It didn't stay that way, though. Boot camp was fine, but after that, things got shit pretty fast. Unlike the recruits of the past–"Join the Army; travel to exotic, distant lands; meet exciting, unusual people, and kill them"–Bogden and Khalil didn't have to go much further than their own backyard to get to the dirty business. The Appalachian Mountains marked the dividing line between the Eastern United States and the roiling mess of rebellion that covered the center of the country, and the friends shipped immediately to West Virginia to start droppin' bodies of their own.

"Maybe it shouldn't, Bog, but this feels different." Khalil's words were half smoke, barely a breath on the night air, but they were heavy all the same.

Bogden sucked on his cigarette as he thought about that. Was it different, really? Was there some line you crossed when you traded carpet bombing for nukes? Or was that a line they'd crossed a long time ago, when they shot their neighbors for saying they'd rather die on their feet than their knees?

Even talking about this was treason. Bogden knew that. He knew Khalil knew that, too. You couldn't ignore orders. And you couldn't secede from the union and get away with it, even if the union didn't want you. Even if they treated you like shit. That was common sense.

"My sister's over there," Bogden said, so quietly he wasn't sure if Khalil would hear him.

"I know."

Bogden's sister was raised in the same dirt as him; coal dust and red clay. It'd made them both desperate in the same sorta hungry way. Like stray dogs, looking for anybody who would promise a square meal and a warm bed. But desperation hit different for women than men.

The lack of options drove Bogden to the Marines,

Khalil by his side. It drove his sister to Kenny from down the road, and that was worse luck. She got a black eye one day and an abortion in a witch's bedroom across the border two days later, and Uncle Sam hadn't let her back in. Ain't no space in the union for whores.

"Did they tell you where you're hitting, yet?" Bogden asked, even though he wasn't sure he wanted to know. He wasn't even sure where Magdalene was. If Khalil told him the bombs were going to hit where she was staying, would Bogden recognize the name?

"There's another briefing in the morning for the details," Khalil responded.

Somehow the lack of an answer wasn't a relief.

"You could..." Bogden didn't dare say the word "desert," but he cut his eyes in the direction of the gate, and he knew Khalil knew what he meant. They were in one of the westernmost outposts of the eastern half of the US–split down the middle as it was by the rebellion spanning from West Virginia to Utah. It was twenty miles tops to the border, which was loosely defined and tenuously held. It would be dangerous to try to get to the autonomous zone, of course, but it wouldn't be impossible. Plenty of guys did it.

But Khalil was shaking his head. He chain-lit another smoke and gave one to Bogden. "They'd just get somebody else to do it," he said reasonably. "Same people would die."

Put so plainly, it sent a chill down Bogden's spine.

The end of everything for Bogden came when Khalil asked if they could take the next night's watch from Hendrix and Gundry, and the answer was, "well, shit boys, don't haveta ask us twice."

Bogden was on a knife's edge all through dinner, waiting to get out there with Khalil, wondering if he was gonna tell him the bombs were headed for his sister after all. He was so messed up over the idea that he didn't even think of the other possibilities until Khalil said, "It's so much worse than we thought."

Turned out it wasn't a nuke threat, like they'd hoped for. A "come crawling back to the union like the scum you are, and we won't blow you to kingdom come" sorta mission. It wasn't a scare tactic, neither. A "we did it once, and we can do it again, so fall in line" thing.

It was an annihilation.

There would be no warning. No opportunities for the rebels to put down their flags and accept the way things were—the real America, not the woke one they'd been dreamin' of before the Grey Uprising. No future where the folks who had run could come back to being treated like shit as Americans, unhappy but alive.

There would be no safe zones. No places folks could retreat to until it was over. Nowhere they could hide their sick, or their elderly, or their babies.

There would be no survivors.

"There's thousands of us," Khalil breathed. "They're workin' with both the Air Force and the Army for more planes, and they're pullin' gunners and bombers from all over. They're hitting *everything*."

This didn't make any sense to Bogden, and he said so. Whatever the rebels might be, whatever they'd done, they were *Americans*. And the autonomous zones used to be states. They could be states again. That meant something, surely. Didn't it?

Khalil shook his head and sucked in smoke from a quivering cigarette. "Nah man, they ain't Americans. Brass ain't told us yet, and they're actin' like we're still fighting, but we've lost the fuckin' war. They don't do this, it's over. America's fuckin' dead."

Khalil pulled his gun on Bogden then. He pointed the muzzle at him, the black metal flat and dull in the fluorescent light at the front of the barracks, and he said, "I'm going, and I won't be back for a couple of hours. I'll try to be back before somebody notices, but if I ain't, I pulled a gun on you. Or I can hit you with it, if you'd rather. Just, please..." His voice cracked and he licked his lips. His eyes shone dark and determined. "Please don't make me shoot you."

The end of everything for Khalil started when he slipped past the guard at the base's gate. It shouldn't have been possible, or at least not as easy as it was, but when you spent five years fighting a brutal war of attrition against your own people, the army you were left with wasn't the best of the best. There'd been plenty of times Khalil had cursed this, pinned down by enemy fire with some incompetent idiot supposed to be covering his back, but tonight he thanked whatever saint looked out for traitors and turncoats for the luck.

It wasn't hard from there to get to the border. He'd grown up poor and bored, so he'd stolen a motorcycle before—he and Bogden used to do it for fun. That and tippin' cows. Back before everything got so fucked up.

The current border line was scarred with trenches and bomb craters, but after he dumped the bike he was able to get past that, too, slipping between the scanning beams of searchlights and holding his breath in fear of dogs.

Once he was past the line, he pulled the white undershirt from his pocket and held it up, creeping forward, his heart hammering so loud he was scared both armies would hear it and fill him full of holes.

This whole area was also mined; he knew that. One wrong step and he and his plan would go up in a shower of dirt and sticky bits of flesh that used to mean something. If he was lucky, nobody would even know he was here, or what he'd tried to do. If he was unlucky, they'd know immediately and go after Bogden.

He was so focused on his feet that he jumped when the mechanical sound of a chamber being racked pierced the stillness. "Stop right there," a voice said.

Quickly lifting his makeshift flag, waving it a bit to make sure the person could see it, Khalil begged the stranger in a harsh whisper not to shoot. The moon was half-choked by clouds, and his hand disappeared in the darkness, but the shirt still had a pale glow to it. He didn't hear any further movement from the blank night around him, but he could hear the person with a gun breathing not far off.

"I'm s'posed to believe that rag?" the voice asked.

It was a woman's voice, Khalil realized now. He'd known that women fought in the rebellion, had shot plenty of them, but it was still jarring.

Khalil chewed his lip. "I've got information."

The woman hesitated before emerging. Then, after patting him down and taking his weapons, she said, "Fine. Come with me. I'll get you through the mines."

She stepped precisely, and Khalil followed her, his heart in his throat. The rebel line was closer than he'd expected. One moment there was empty darkness, and the next, the woman was putting out a hand to keep him from stumbling into the thicket of thorns the grease-smeared rebels were using as cover.

"He says he has intel," his guard said to a gaunt man who had stepped out of the darkness with a rifle.

The man jerked his head, and the woman continued to lead Khalil.

The rebels hadn't dug trenches like the Americans had. The Americans were facing constant low-grade fire and intermittent land-based attacks, thrown back in time by the rebels' lack of access to technology and forced to fortify accordingly. The rebels, though, were facing the most advanced military of all time. Their camp was stealth-based and mobile; all light cover and jumpy sentries.

Khalil found the commander of this detachment in a stolen American tank, piled with branches to look like part of the landscape from above. It was cramped inside, and the woman who had escorted him didn't follow down the hatch, leaving him to face the commander alone.

After five years in this war, Khalil should have learned not to have expectations. But he was still surprised to find himself looking at the dark, wrinkled face of someone who could be his grandmother. She had a warm face and fierce eyes, and when she looked at him, Khalil was very glad he'd never had the opportunity to try to shoot her.

"Val says you have information, and that you seemed serious about it," the old woman said.

She didn't give her name, and Khalil supposed it didn't matter. Whoever she was, she would either listen to him now, or she'd be dead tomorrow. Maybe she'd be dead tomorrow either way.

"They're planning on nuking you." He'd intended to say it more smoothly than that. More convincingly, or at least more gently. But here in this tank, with all the communications ripped out and the wires reaching from the walls like roots from a forgotten potato, the words just spilled out. "All of you, up as close to the border as they can get without hitting themselves. Tomorrow. They're not going to give a warning. They're just going to flatten the whole interior."

The commander didn't respond right away. At first, she didn't even react. The air inside the captured tank went very still, and very cold, and if it wasn't for the frantic hammering of his heart and the relentless, all-consuming ache it left in his chest, Khalil would have thought that time itself had frozen.

Then the commander rearranged her hands in her lap, folding them calmly and primly, like she was a young girl preparing for prayer. "I see."

Khalil tried to swallow and was surprised to find he couldn't. At some point tears had begun running down his face, and he only noticed when he felt them slide wetly down his chin and start to collect in the hollows above his collarbone.

"When is this happening?" the commander asked.

"O' seven hundred." He checked his watch. It was three in the morning. "I've gotta get back, or they'll know what I've done. I'm going to be on one of the planes." He put his fist to his mouth and felt green for a minute but then managed to swallow. "I have to be, or they'll wonder why I'm not."

The commander nodded, already reaching for the hatch of the tank. "Okay," she said. "Then we'd better make sure you get there."

When they reached the fortifications, Khalil made to duck back into the darkness again, but the commander snagged his sleeve. He turned, afraid she'd changed her mind.

"What's your name?" she asked. "I want to make sure our people remember it."

The corner of his lips twitched in a grim smile, and the woman who was to lead him back through the mines waited as he said, "Khalil. Khalil Rucker."

The end of everything for the United States started when they sent out 5,000 planes, and one of them had Khalil Rucker in the bomber's seat.

They flew out at exactly 07:00, after assembling on the tarmac at 05:00; just forty minutes after Khalil slipped back onto base and into his place beside Bogden on watch.

Khalil stared at the warheads as they flew. They were smaller than he'd thought they'd be. Twelve of them, lined up and gleaming like plastic eggs on Easter Sunday, except they were all decorated the same way. Army green and mustard yellow, stamped with the bold US stencil that was supposed to fill Khalil with something resembling patriotic fervor when he saw it.

Khalil couldn't see what they were flying over, but by how long they'd been in the plane, he expected they must be over rebel territory. He wondered if it was fortifications and supply lines below, or if it was houses. Children. Birthday parties.

The inner reaches of the autonomous zone had been more or less quiet for years. There were bombings, of course, but not like on the border. Most of the interior was less like an active warzone and more like a new country of its own, no matter what the press releases from the US government said. They were just normal people, living their lives and trying not to think too much about the war, just like everybody else. Khalil knew that.

"T minus five to drop," said the voice in Khalil's headset. He was sweating so much in his fatigues that he felt like he was in a wetsuit. He moved to the row of warheads and checked them over, making sure everything was ready. Making sure everything was as it should be, when nothing was as it should be.

There were six men in the plane: the pilot and copilot, separated from the rest of the crew by the cockpit doors; then the flight engineer; the navigator; and two bombardiers. Khalil was the primary, and Arnold Jenkins was here in case Khalil didn't end up having the stomach for it.

"Thirty seconds," said the voice in Khalil's headset. He put his hand on the trigger and looked into the bombsight. Everything was topography and measurements, not showing him what he was about to hit or who he was about to kill, but he knew that if it was worth hitting, it had to be big.

The commander had believed him. She'd started warning her people even as she was escorting Khalil back to no-man's-land, and they'd run with the news.

"It's been a hell of a long war," she'd told him. "Most people have some sort of bomb shelter they'll hopefully be able to get to." Then she'd put her hand on his shoulder and said, "You're a hero. Thank you for what you've done for us."

"Fire at will," the voice in the headset said now.

Khalil took a deep breath, his thumb sweaty where it rested on the button. He pictured the commander, and Bogden's sister, and every guy he'd ever known to leave his bunk empty in the middle of the night and make a break for the border.

"Fire at will," the voice repeated.

Khalil Rucker turned, jaw set, and shot the second bombardier.

The end of everything for the old world was well on its way by the time they shot Khalil Rucker.

A nuke from the hijacked plane had hit an American battalion between the border and Washington, D.C., but the plane was forced down before it could loose the rest of its payload. And even though the news covered Rucker's breakdown like he was the second coming of Benedict Arnold, overall, the splash to the brass was minimal. Sure, he'd killed a lot of soldiers, but what use were rag-tag, battle-weary soldiers now?

The war was over, and hazmat-suited construction crews were already rolling over the scarred ground of no-man's-land, putting up the most secure fence modern technology could provide. Eighteen-foot-tall electric paneling, strong enough to fry you crispy, topped with sparking razor-wire, created a barrier between the United States and the nuclear obliteration it had made of the rebels. Just in case anyone who had been close enough to the border to survive got the bright idea that they wanted to come back now.

As for Khalil, he stood stiff-backed and somber in front of a different wall, the concrete behind him bullet-eaten and brain-spattered. His face was tearstained, but he wasn't crying anymore. There was a swollen lump on his temple, the bruising creeping dark towards his eye, and he held his chin up proudly. He had a secret worth dying for, and he intended to do so.

Bogden was in the crowd, and the two friends locked eyes for the last time over the heads of the firing squad. Khalil tried to communicate with his mind that it had worked, that people in the interior had gone to ground, that the US had lost the war it thought it won, but of course, Bogden couldn't hear him.

The gunshots split the air with a violent crack, and Bogden couldn't help but flinch. Khalil's body slumped immediately, the back of his skull blasted out. His dreams were a spray of red across the concrete, but his secrets died with him.

When the dust of nations settled, it found Magdalene, her rebel husband, and their infant daughter in a bunker, along with their elderly neighbors, a young deserter, and a dog. The old man had sprained his ankle running to the ladder, but it was minor, and they were all in as good of spirits as could be expected. The radio in the corner predicted that cleanup could begin in just a few days—long before the canned goods started to dwindle.

Leaning back against the wall in heavy-limbed exhaustion, Magdalene ran her fingers through her baby's hair. Little bits of concrete and dirt were still caught in the downy strands, loosed from the ceiling during the barrage. But she was alive—they all were—and it was over.

"Thank you, Khalil." Magdalene whispered. She prayed his ghost could hear her.

Old White Guy is Calm as the World Burns

by Brian U. Garrison

Defeat cannot reach the center
of a mind behind a blame thrower.
Flammable poisons ignite, flare,
and flash past visibility. Stepping
over a bundle of tarps and bungees

fires up the imagination, cooking
visions of theft. The spicy pungence
from an unshowered body burns
the nose and deludes the onlooker:
Look how the system has been cheated.

Rainwater and starvation are a choice,
says the brain. A bystander's stare torches
the last scrap of shelter, and even
the person under the tarp, like the smog,
sloughs toward periphery, invisible

as the distant city horizons. Striking matches,
candle bearers light up the night. Sequins
against the curtain. If the blame thrower
glows bright enough, the city sparkles.
Undefeatable, if you're in the right mind.

Le Coyote

by M. K. Martin

"What's French for 'coyote'?" Kaydence asked. She rubbed her hands together, watching the little cloud of her breath spiral away into the night sky. The air was so cold the inside of her nose hurt. As did her butt from sitting so long in the plastic lawn chair behind an abandoned gas station in the middle of East Jesus Nowhere.

"Don't know," Alex said. They paced along the side of the building to stare down the road again. "Probably le coyote."

"So, you're Le Coyote?" Kaydence called after them.

Alex glanced back and held up a finger to their lips.

"What? There's no one out here for miles and miles." Kaydence couldn't keep the whine out of her voice. She was exhausted from being scared. She was freezing, probably already had hypothermia, and she had to pee. Again.

Alex came back, stomping their feet, and leaned against the wall beside Kaydence. They had been waiting since one of Alex's friends—an older woman sporting handknit mittens, hat, and scarf—had dropped them off just before sunset. Kaydence didn't have any way to keep track of time because part of the instructions was to leave all her electronics at home. No phone, no watch, not even her new ID card because of the chip in it.

"Know how when you call the cable repair guy, and they give you a window of time from tomorrow at 7 a.m. until the breaking of the world, and you have to be there? This is like that. We just have to be here."

"Cable repair person," Kaydence said with a smirk.

"Yeah, sure, call out my subconscious sexism," Alex said. "Thanks."

"Just trying to help you live your values." Kaydence flipped her long blond hair over her shoulder innocently.

"I am," Alex said. "Otherwise, I wouldn't be out here with you of all people."

"You of all people? Is that like a 'you people' thing?" Kaydence leaned forward.

Bickering with Alex provided a welcome distraction from being worried 24/7 for the past month and a half. Ever since the day of the pink plus sign.

"Who would that even be?" Alex tucked their hands into their armpits. "Oh, I forgot how historically disadvantaged the children of rich and powerful white cishet politicians are. Let me alert the rest of Antifa so we can add you to our list of protected classes."

"And yet, here you are, freezing your ass off with me."

"Because I am living my values," they said. "Doesn't mean I have to like you or anything that you stand for."

"What I stand for? What does that mean?"

But before Alex could answer, the faint rumble of a car engine sounded in the distance. It grew steadily louder. Kaydence pressed her back against the wall of the gas station. Only three kinds of people used this road: loggers and miners accessing the newly opened Boundary Waters Canoe Area Wilderness; ICE agents looking for illegals crossing the border; and illegals . . . like her.

Alex clicked off their flashlight and went to the corner of the gas station's back wall where they could peek around to the road. Kaydence watched them, trying to see from their reaction which of the three this car was.

As the engine sound grew louder, Alex crouched down and slowly leaned back, keeping out of the beam of the headlights. Kaydence covered her mouth with both hands, even though she knew it was silly. No way could anyone in the car hear her breathing. Still.

The car drove past, and Alex crept back to her. Their face was pale, eyes wide.

"ICE," they said.

Kaydence shuddered. The only thing worse than having to sneak into Canada would be getting caught trying to sneak into Canada. She didn't even want to imagine the kind of trouble that would cause. Not just for her. She would be sent to one of the Nurturing Centers in Texas until the baby came, then face a trial for attempted murder. But while she picked vegetables and fruit and memorized Bible verses and was monitored on behalf of whoever was going to adopt her baby, her dad would lose his post. The Family First party would quietly shuffle him out of the way and scrub his name off their records as if he had never existed at all.

No job meant no house for her family, no school for her little brother, no insulin for her mom.

"What now? We have to go, right? We can't stay here." Kaydence got up and looked around. Pine forest far as the eye could see in every direction except the ribbon of the road.

"I don't know," Alex said. They pulled out an old timey style pocket watch and clicked on their flashlight long enough to read it. "We're still in the window. We should stay here. They'll come."

"What if they don't?" Kaydence squinted down the road. Was that faint red glow of taillights getting brighter? Had ICE stopped? Were they coming back?

"Calm down," Alex said.

"Seriously?" Kaydence glared. "When in the history of calming down has anyone ever calmed down because someone said, 'Calm down.'? Nah-ev-er."

White lights, not red.

"They're turning around," Alex said.

Kaydence shook her head. Of course they were going to get caught. She wasn't lucky.

She never had been. God was punishing her for letting Gunner do sex to her. Now her whole family would suffer. Hot tears stung her eyes. "I would be better off dead."

"No." Alex grabbed Kaydence's hand. "I know you don't trust me, and I don't like you, like not even a little for a variety of reasons but listen. I'm going to get you over the border. I promise."

"How?"

"Go into the trees, at least three or four trunks in. Look back after each tree and make sure you can see the gas station. Find something to hide behind. Stay there until I come get you or someone calls for Jane."

"Jane?"

"Yeah, that's what we call you all: The Janes. Like Jane Roe." Alex looked over their shoulder. The headlights were clearly visible. "Hurry!" They squeezed Kaydence's hand then gave her a little push towards the dark wall of trees.

Crossing the patch of tall grass and weeds between the gas station and the woods took about a million years with the car's engine roaring like a dragon behind her, but Kaydence didn't look back. She couldn't. Inside the forest the dark squeezed around her, trying to suffocate her.

She stumbled over roots, fumbled through pricker bushes.

A car door slammed, and she threw herself down like she was doing an active shooter drill at school. She covered her head with her arms and sobbed into the frozen ground. Her breath melted the frost, making the ground slimy under her.

"What are you doing out here?" The man's voice carried clearly through the still night.

"Fuck off, Gestapo goon." Alex's voice.

"Sounds like resisting arrest to me," said another man. "What do you think, Easton?"

"You can't arrest me," Alex said. "I'm an American."

"Don't look like one," said Easton. "Let's see your ID."

"Let's see your warrant."

"Don't need one to detain an illegal," the second man said. "Get in the van. They can sort you out at Carlton."

"Hey!" Easton yelled. Kaydence turned her head, her cheek against the wet, moldy leaves, and looked back at the road. A flicker across the ICE van's headlights as Alex darted away. Easton charged after them. The other man went around the back of the van to corner Alex between them.

For a few minutes, all Kaydence could hear was the ICE agents' puffing and cursing. Just as she was beginning to think Alex might be luckier than she, Easton shouted triumphantly, then a flat, hard smack like her brother hitting his punching bag.

Easton and the other ICE agent came back to the van, dragging Alex between them.

Easton pushed them against the van with his arm across their neck. Alex started choking.

The other ICE agent handed Easton a pair of plastic zip cuffs, which he put on Alex's wrists before he stepped back. Alex slid down the van and fell over onto their side, gasping and wheezing to catch their breath.

"What's your name?" Easton asked.

"Name? Better start with sex," the other agent said.

"Are you a girl or boy?"

"I'm a fucking adult, so neither." Alex sounded horse.

"Check?" East said.

"Check." The other agent pushed Alex onto their back and knelt over them with a knee on their shoulder. He unzipped their coat and pulled it open, reached inside.

Alex grunted, then squealed in pain. Kaydence closed her eyes and covered her ears.

"Girl," the agent said, his voice muffled through Kaydence's hands.

"Put her in the van," Easton said. "I'm starving. Let's go get some grub."

The doors slammed. The engine grew louder as the car accelerated away, back towards town. Kaydence lay on the ground until her bladder couldn't take it any longer. Shivering all over, she pulled down her jeans and peed, trying not to think of sniffer dogs tracking pregnant people by the hormones in their pee.

Was it too late to go back? She didn't even know where the nearest town was. She would probably freeze to death walking along the road. She should have turned herself in. At least then Alex might have been able to escape.

But if she went back, she would have to explain to her parents what had happened, would have to go to the Nurturing Center. Her dad would still probably lose his job, and her family would still be ruined. She refused to think about being pregnant, about giving birth, about how her aunt had died from complications after her cousin was born.

Gunner had told her she couldn't get pregnant her first time, and she believed him. She pressed her palms into her eyes and screamed silently. She didn't want to die, but if she did, her family would be safe, especially if they never found her body. Maybe she should start walking to Canada?

Another car on the road. Kaydence ducked down behind the nearest tree, watching the headlights approach. The car didn't slow and as it got closer, she could see it was a logging truck. She remembered her aunt making a posterboard sign to protest logging in the Boundary Waters. It used to be some kind of nature preserve or something. But everyone knew it was important to do forest management by taking out the big old trees. There was a movie about that she'd seen at school explaining that once the old growth forests were gone, the forest fires would stop. And who didn't want that?

Kaydence huddled by the tree, too cold to stay, too tired to go. More headlights. Let it be ICE coming back. She would give herself up.

The car stopped in front of the gas station.

"Hello? Jane?" a woman's voice.

"Me!" Kaydence clambered to her feet and hurried towards the gas station. "That's me."

The woman got back in the car and turned it around, then got out again. As Kaydence emerged from the forest, the woman looked around carefully. "Is anyone with you?"

"ICE took Alex," Kaydence blurted out. She fell into

the passenger's seat and held her hands over the air vent, relishing the heat even though her fingers ached and tingled.

The woman got in. She was in her mid-thirties and looked like any of the moms from church or school. She didn't look like a liberal–no piercings or face tattoos or Satanic icons in her car.

"We'll deal with that later," the woman said. "I'm Sofia. Let's get you to Canada."

Kaydence wouldn't have believed she could sleep after everything that had happened, but next thing she knew, Sofia was gently shaking her. She opened her eyes. The car was stopped alongside a one-lane gravel road. The sky was barely lightening, but it was clearly morning.

"We walk from here," Sofia said. "It's only three miles."

"Where are we?" Kaydence rubbed the crusties out of her eyes and looked around.

"Probably best if you don't worry about that," Sofia said. "Keeps us all safer, right?"

Kaydence nodded, thinking about the way Alex had cried out when the ICE agents caught them. She was sure she would never be able to forget that awful sound. She shuddered.

Sofia got out of the car and stretched. Kaydence copied her. She felt stiff and sore all over. The front of her coat was caked with a thin layer of mud and a few old, brown leaves. She looked like one of those homeless veterans the police chased out of parks and away from coffee shops. Mom said not to give them money because they would just spend it on drugs.

"Here." Sofia handed her a thermos and a peanut butter and jelly sandwich. "Let's go."

They walked through the dawn and into the morning. Sofia seemed to know where she was going, only checking her compass twice. After an hour or so they came out of the woods and crossed some frost-covered fields, leaving dark footprints in the white crusted grasses. They came to a split rail fence, like a history exhibit, and climbed over, then walked down another dirt road. It led to a farmhouse with smoke coming out of the chimney.

A young man, only a few years older than Gunner, waited near a battered pickup truck.

He nodded to Sofia and opened the door for Kaydence.

"If anyone asks, you're my fiancée," he said with a slight accent.

"I should probably know your name then," Kaydence said.

"Julian. And you'll be Madeline, small, but brave, eh?"

Kaydence got into the truck and waved to Sofia as Julian drove away. Three hours later she was at a clinic.

She was surprised by how fast everything happened. She read the consent form and signed it, then the nurse practitioner took her back to the exam room where he did a final check to confirm how far along the pregnancy was. Less than fifteen minutes later, everything was done.

Kaydence took the pain pills and didn't complain when Julian came to pick her up after.

Sofia walked her back to the car, which was uncomfortable, but no worse than really bad period cramps. She had to change her pad before they got in the car. Sofia gave her a hot water bottle. She sat in the passenger's seat, watching the trees flash by, trying to believe it was all over.

She would go home, tell her parents she'd had a wonderful time at her friend's house, and life would be back to normal.

As they passed the abandoned gas station, Kaydence sat up. She wanted to do something to help Alex. They had sacrificed a lot to help her, even if she was one of those people.

"My dad's office coordinates with ICE," she said. "If I can get their schedules, would that help get Alex out?"

"It would," Sofia said. She looked at Kaydence thoughtfully. "But you could do more, if you were interested."

Deep inside her, Kaydence felt the fear that had taken root when she stared at the little pink plus sign transmuting into something else, something wild, even dangerous. She was furious.

"I'm interested."

Great Again?

by Desiree Batiste

Twice the promise has been
Make America Great Again
Eye-opening to think anyone
has seen greatness in us
In the beginning, religious persecution
by pilgrims who fled to find freedom
Calvinist Protestant was the only way
We protected our new country
by taking it from those already living here
Was that our greatness?
We established laws which were intended
to protect our equality
Whoops! Guess we forgot about women
and Blacks, too
Somehow, the fact that we saw them as less
made it true?
We learned nothing from the Civil War
which almost tore our new country apart

Those who still sit in silence
waiting for the South to rise again
Was that our greatness?
Hate rose with hoods and crosses
Black Americans live in fear
We ended segregation
but not the hate and fear that drove it in
the first place
Was that our greatness?
Men make health care laws
for women
Projecting their religious beliefs onto us
It has nothing to do with them
It isn't even their bodies!
But we have the increasingly loud voices
demanding
more religious edicts
Marriage is only allowed between
a man and a woman
Some states in their wisdom try to
force women to stay in marriages
by banning divorce
and give the decision of if and when
children will be had
to the men
Just like that... we lost our rights to
abortion, ending toxic marriages, and
autonomy over our own bodies!
Is this the greatness of which he spoke?
We're ostriches with our heads in the sand
There are only two genders

because they won't acknowledge anything
that doesn't match this revelation
And DEI doesn't exist, because they say it
doesn't
LGBTQ who?
Our population keeps shrinking
because all these people vanished in the
eyes of those
who swore to dedicate themselves to
representing us
Climate change isn't real, he declares,
so the planet better stop threatening to
make our lives unpleasant!
The dictator's word is law
The courts cannot knock down these
orders
fast enough to stop what's already started
Social Security is a scam, they say,
ripe with fraud
Meanwhile, these billionaires cutting 'waste'
are getting rid of funds for education
disease research
Laughing as they watch the price of
groceries skyrocket
Laughing as they fire workers who have
families
or those about to retire
Laughing as LA burns to the ground
They look down upon the pile of money
the government has now
and say 'it is good'

They watch us struggle
like beetles on their backs
poising their magnifying glasses above us
The sizzle sears
but no more tears
"We've decided that you don't feel pain
You must love what we've done with the
place!"
Every heartbreaking decision has the
MAGA stamp of approval
as the toadies cheer
the Proud Boys nod
and the Nazi salute flies under the radar
past all those in denial
More book bans coming
Media under control to shape the narrative
Truth in reporting, no more
How long before movie bans?
Or the government dictating what movies
can be made?
Gun rights? Those will be going soon
No chance of rebellion against
The New World Order
when we are armed only with sadness
in our broken hearts
and the question
as we look around our new wasteland
bleeding out the few freedoms we did
fight for
Is this the greatness you promised?

Lying In Wait

by Rick M. Cook

A massive crowd gathers at the east end of the National Mall, eager to get this public spectacle underway. Fortunately, the fresh spring weather has held, encouraging over a million people to attend. The night skies are clear except for the drones flying overhead, projecting images of the gorgeous cherry blossoms along the Potomac shot earlier in the day. Behind us, the U.S. Capitol basks in bright spotlights, and the beauty of this perfect April evening gives me hope.

Sitting beside me on the raised dais, my second-in-command wrings her hands. Tiny twitches in her fingers betray her restless energy. "Deirdre," I say. "It's going to be okay. He can't touch us."

Deirdre Hurley, a rail-thin health nut, is paler than normal this evening. A lean scaffold of muscle carved from Athenian-like discipline, "Dedicated Deirdre" brings a crazy work ethic to Washington. Her sinewy frame has less to do with the kale smoothies and more to do with her devotion to the job. But her agitated state is rubbing off on me now. I can't show fear, not tonight, not here.

"I know, Marcus," she says to me. "But President Tass is so spiteful and vindictive. And his diehard cultists? They freak me out. I've had, like, fifty death threats just this week."

"I get it," I say, using my most soothing politician's voice. Power in the hands of the arrogant and ignorant is never a good thing. "Just remember, we're acting within our constitutional authority. He can't touch us. We're doing the right thing."

She drops her eyes. "Even if it means being killed by one of his lunatic followers?"

I turn in my seat to half-face her. "Would you rather live under another dictator?"

Thirty years ago, my Deputy Secretary was born as our democracy was toppled from the inside. She wouldn't remember the subsequent food and fuel shortages nor the forced rationing of everything from bullets to blankets to bananas, much less the vitriol between state governments blaming each other for America's downfall. She wouldn't remember how the reckless Benedict Arnold of that time told lie upon lie, driving wedges between America's factions. His divide-and-conquer strategy worked, and it placed him atop the smoldering remains of a once-stellar democracy.

But I remember.

Back then, my parents could afford a three-bedroom apartment as federal employees before the mass firings. I had dreams of owning a house and car before the subsequent seventy-percent inflation hit us, pushing everything but the basics out of reach. I remember when we could walk down the street without worry of being arrested on phony charges, forced to show identification, or worse, shot by the National Guard for being out after curfew. I remember a Congress with a spine, before it was abolished by a petty and petulant *dick*-tator.

Even as a twenty-something back then, I saw the daily dumbing down of Americans by wealthy conservatives who spent billions to push false narratives, paying fascist puppets to shout fake news and outrageous accusations without evidence from their social media platforms and "news" feeds. They flooded the zone, trough-feeding the masses with so-called "truth bombs," heaped servings of lies and half-truths gobbled down at the all-you-can-eat buffet of bullshit.

The more insane the conspiracy theory, the more the uneducated and low-info voters consumed them. Why? Because believing bullshit is so much easier and more entertaining than having to think and reason.

Those who voted for the "faux-king idiot" that brought down American democracy later admitted they were less inclined to study how government works than watch hideously large trucks bash each other in mock battle. With ridiculous promises of a better life filling their heads, they didn't have to think. Just sacrifice a bit more unchecked power to the liars and cheaters. And they believed it all... right up until America's Second Civil War erupted.

I knew then what my life's mission had to be: provide politics with more honesty.

"No," Deirdre says, "I've heard enough from my

parents and grandparents about the Second Civil War. My NIPAR implant filled in the rest. I want none of that misery, the insecurity and lies of a crazy dictator, the public execut—"

Her face freezes and blanches as if she'd walked in on me sitting on the commode. "I'm sorry, sir. I... I didn't mean—"

"It's okay, Deirdre." I pat her arm to let her know I'm not offended. "He did what he thought was right. Just as we're doing today."

A tear forms in the corner of her eye. "I never met him, but I loved your father. Everybody did." She dabs at the tear. "He was such a great man, a true American hero."

Now, it's my turn to hold back a tear. "Thank you, Deirdre."

"Yes, sir," she says. "I was too little to remember it, but my NIPAR tells me his death was the spark the Resistance needed to take back the country."

I'm glad I don't have one of those 'nips' installed in my head. *How can she sleep with that neural implant babbling on in her brain?*

When I return to the present, Deirdre is comparing my father to Che Guevara and singing praises of my father's crusade, the work I carry on today.

"... his sham of an arrest in the middle of the night for being a *dissident...*" She hooks two fingers in the air. "All shameful paranoia of a shameless and corrupt president."

And now, I think, *we are faced with the rise of another wannabe despot.*

An awkward silence falls between us. After a bit, she

huffs. "He's late. He has no respect for us or for those that serve this country."

Again, I pat her arm to calm those nerves. "Don't worry, Deirdre. He'll show. He's been bragging about this showdown for months. A no-show would demonstrate to everyone the liar and coward he's always been."

Deirdre chuckles. "They'll know soon enough."

In the distance, the white marble of the Lincoln Memorial gleams under dazzling lights, and a pride swells within me. If he had the technology, Honest Abe would do as much as Deirdre and I have done to keep this nation united and save it from yet another divisive war.

"So many people are truth-blind," Deirdre says, almost as if to herself. "You present them with the facts, and they'll still only believe what they want to believe."

Maria Menendez, our moderator and one of the most respected journalists in America, steps onto the dais. "POTUS will arrive in five minutes." We nod to her as she takes her seat in the leather wingback between our chairs and those reserved for President Tass and VP Derek Lictendum.

A full forty minutes later, Marine One flies in low over the crowd, sending blankets and cups and protest signs fluttering in a naked, thundering display of the power behind another would-be king. He was supposed to land near the Garfield Memorial and be shuttled over, but the helicopter touches down on the Mall, forcing some of the crowd to scramble for cover.

"What a childish ass," I mutter.

Deirdre nods and points at the protestors. "That's why their signs list Tass's name with a lowercase 't' and a capital 'A.' To highlight his *tiny* brain and the *huge* Ass that he is."

"Oh? Guess I've been too busy to notice," I lie.

"Sure," she says, smirking. "It's less insulting than the other moniker for Franklin Albert Tass: 'FAT Ass.' That's my fave."

Despite the serious nature of this public meeting, I laugh out loud.

Soon, we're joined onstage by President Tass and VP Lictendum. The two look like they've stepped out of the Jack Sprat nursery rhyme.

The Veep—a.k.a. Jack Sprat—is "Doormat Derek" Lictendum. Almost as thin as Deirdre, he was chosen for his lack of experience and wit, never to question his would-be king. Derek's cheesy lip-curling snarl—no doubt misappropriated from some cartoon villain—is rumored to be the side effect of his current job. Late-night comedy hosts dubbed him "PAK-man," the Presidential Ass Kisser. But it's tiresome for the rest of us, evidence of his contempt for the law and our entire system of self-governance.

By contrast, "Sticky Fingers" Franklin Tass is a well-marbled, seventy-six-year-old man with gray hair as thin as his skin. He's got all seven deadly sins locked down tighter than my quantum-computing servers. Short at five feet seven with a belt straining somewhere under a huge beer gut, Tass's 350-pound physique is the epitome of greed and gluttony. His brooding nature, overbearing brow, and stooped shoulders contribute to his overall *l'essence de Néandertal.*

His disdain for the law is exactly why I stayed in politics, despite being ready to retire.

Tass's all-night ragers are notorious, especially the madness of the infamous Easter Weekend Meltdown last year, after which world leaders threatened to send him their best psychiatrists. Most NIPAR broadcasts have banned him because only the most sex-craved cretins can stand to experience the unchecked, lascivious thoughts that brew in that cesspool he calls a brain. Worst of all, he's lazier than a dormant volcano, claiming credit for others' work and passing the buck so often it's got more frequent flyer miles than Air Force One.

Host Maria Menendez explains the rules of our discourse and then introduces us. We move to our separate trenches, and the political tug-o-war commences.

Maria scans her digipad and begins. "President Tass, you've called to have your acting secretary of the Department of Political Accountability—or DOPA—arrested and thrown in jail. However, the law as stated in the Twenty-eighth Amendment, adopted after the previous overthrow of our democracy, clearly states in Section 2, Paragraph 2, and I quote: 'The Secretary or Deputy Secretary of DOPA—both duly elected officials—cannot be removed from office by the sitting president or any congressional member or action of Congress. Sec-

DOPA must finish the assigned ten-year term unless retirement, death, incapacity, or impeachment renders them unable to do so. In exchange for this limited immunity, Sec-DOPA can never be elected President or Vice President.'"

Maria looks up from her notes. "In light of this law, how can you, President Tass, justify your call for Secretary Davidson's arrest or dismissal?"

Tass shifts his weight like a bag of bricks and points a finger at me. "Well, just look at 'im! He's clearly not capable of doing any kind of software development. I mean, have you ever seen a Black guy code anything? He can't do it!"

Shock spreads across Maria's normally placid face. "President Tass, are you suggesting his race has some influence over his capacity to—"

"Maria, it's okay," I interject. "Let's stay on topic and not chase the race-baiting down any rat holes. I'm okay with his racism."

Tass scoots to the edge of his seat and gestures with both hands. "I'm not the racist! You're the racist, telling all those lies about me."

"The only lies told have been told by you, sir."

Grunting, the president struggles to his feet, nonchalantly turns off his mic, and finger guns me as he walks past. He whispers, "You're going to Gitmo in a body bag, pal."

Mic back on, Tass moves to center stage. "Forget that fool," he says to the crowd, jerking a thumb at me.

"Mr. President, let's keep to the rules," instructs Maria. "Please retake your seat."

"I will not!" He struts back and forth across the stage,

cock of the walk, his back to us. Overhead, a thousand drones—each equipped with a small, lightweight LED screen—cluster to project his live image in a mosaic across the night sky. Together, they form one giant, ominous floating head. "They came to see *me*," he shouts. "Not that loser."

Many boo him, but a significant number of his supporters cheer him on.

"Please, Mr. President," Maria pleads.

He ignores her. "I've done many great things for this country. So many great things. The economy? Skyrocketing! The middle class? Thriving! Inflation's so whipped, it's not even in the dictionary anymore. Unemployment? Dead like the Department of Education. Stocks are soaring because I briefly eliminated gravity. You're welcome."

"Sir, none of that is true," corrects Maria.

Tass steamrolls over her words, too absorbed in his own to notice—or care. "I moved Taco Tuesdays to Fridays because who doesn't need an easy meal at the end of the work week, huh? And in the White House, I got rid of math. Nobody liked it, nobody needed it. That *al-Gee-Bra*? It's a *Muslim* conspiracy designed to confuse us! It was holding back the American Dream. It's gone now. Everybody is thrilled! All because of me."

"Sir," Maria says again, "that's preposterous."

He turns and glares at the journalist. That's when I see the TruthBar for the first time outside the lab. The horizontal bar's dark outline flashes on Tass's forehead and fills in with color. Like mercury in a thermometer, the color bar quickly pushes from "Clear True Blue" through "Minted Truth" green, blows past the bright yellow of "Slippery Banana," and finally settles on the toasty orange of "Cheezgasm." The final touch is the text "67% LIE" overlaid on the bar.

He's officially wandered into brainwashing territory.

I don't care for the goofy color labels Marketing suggested, but they give us some DEFCON-esque levels to work with.

After a few seconds, the meter's bioluminescence fades. If it weren't for the stunned silence of a few onlookers, I would've thought no one saw it.

Tass stiffens. "Are you calling me a liar, Ms. Menendez?"

Lap dog Derek dutifully jumps to his boss's defense, moving to stand behind him, obedient and obsequious. "How dare you, madam! Unlike you, we've *always* told the American people the truth."

There it is again, but more evident in Derek's pasty forehead—the flash of his TruthBar's outline, color instantly spiking to a mucky brownish red, overlaid with text reading "94% LIE."

Maria hesitates, squinting at Derek. But his TruthBar must've faded before she could read it because she only shakes her head and sighs. "No one is calling either of you a liar."

"Not yet," Deirdre mutters.

"Good thing," Tass says with a threatening grin. "Don't wanna have to put you and your entire network in time-out now, would we?"

He doesn't wait for an answer but turns back to the audience. "I've got big plans, such hugely plans, plans like nobody's ever—ya know, we're cutting the flag poles in half. Did you know that? That way when we have to fly flags at half-mast, they'll already be there. Saves time. So much time..."

My God, how in the hell did such an idiot ever get elected?

Drone-projected in the sky, Tass's bloated face pulses with color across his brow. The meter only rises halfway to goldenrod, the "Slippery Banana" level.

He blathers on. "Speaking of poles, I'm ordering all solar panels be built on *extendable* poles. That way, when the sun goes down, ya know, *over* the horizon, they can still reach those delicious rays. 'They go up, they go down, we get electricity all around.' That's my new campaign slogan. Like it? Doesn't take a genius to know *that's* smart."

A giggle escapes Deirdre. "Sure doesn't," she says, rolling her eyes.

I watch for the TruthBar on POTUS's forehead, but nothing displays. "Gotta glitch," I mumble, "cuz *that* can't be true, can it?" Deirdre says nothing but makes a note.

I catch Maria's attention, raise my eyebrows, and gesture for her to cut him off. She holds up a finger but allows the idiot to continue... for ratings purposes, probably.

Fine, bury yourself, Mr. President.

"Or maybe," Tass continues, "we'll do gasoline-powered solar panels. Who knows?"

Deirdre snorts while I groan.

Erraticus Maximus plows ahead. "I got genetic engineers designing a new national bird for America. A better bird, a glorious bird, an eagle like one you've never seen. It'll be the—no, not one of those *transgender* eagles. No, no. The scientists will build a new eagle out of little eagle blocks. And when it spreads its wings, you'll see *my* face in its feathers. It'll be so beautiful, you'll want to kiss it."

Again, the TruthBar doesn't display. *Is it broken or—holy shit—are they really wasting money on such a project?*

"You look up," Tass continues, "and you'll see me watching over you. So beautiful. I'm calling it the *PatriEagle*. Or maybe the *PartyEagle*, I'm not sure which. It's a big decision, ya know, one of my biggest. But isn't that incredible? Just like my brain, incredible. It'll be—"

PAK-man Derek, his face in a rictus of childlike glee, interrupts his boss. "Oh! Oh! Tell them about Mount Everest."

With both hands, Tass pulls his pants up while trying to suck in his gut, and I'm suddenly reminded of the Hindenburg disaster.

"Thanks, Derek, for the, um..., Oh, yeah. We're gonna dismantle Mount Everest brick by brick and move it to Kansas. By trains, planes, maybe even submarines. Why? Because why should—where is it located again, Derek? Oh yeah, right—why should Japan have the world's tallest mountain when America is the best country ever? Let's make the Great Plains greater!"

Sweet Jesus, did Hamilton and Madison really think the Electoral College was the best way forward?

Again, I glare at Ms. Menendez, my eyebrows on fire. She does the *wait-a-minute finger* thing again. But Tass is building to something, and I've got to stop it. This is *my* meeting, *my* announcement. I rise from my chair, move forward, and prepare to take the reins back.

But the audience clamor lowers in pitch, and the nays finally overtake the yeas. I halt mid-step, hoping he's finally poked the wrong bear.

Unfazed, Tass doubles down. "Oh, don't you worry. We're not raising your taxes."

Tass's truth meter bolts to life and pegs into the crimson of "Pants on Fire" with a "100% LIE" readout. In both cheeks, an additional image of George Washington appears and facepalms himself.

Excellent. We've achieved the software's Bonus Round.

Unaware of his lies being exposed, Tass rolls on. "I gotta new agency gonna handle all the funding. It's called the Federal Reallocation for Asset Utilization and Distribution."

I move forward and switch my mic back on. "You realize, Mr. President, that its acronym would be FRAUD..."

He gazes back at me, coming up to his side, and stumbles. A bewildered look washes across his face, almost as if he'd forgotten I'd been behind him the whole time. He shakes his head dismissively. "Doesn't matter. They said the name wouldn't test well. But I like it!"

He turns back to the crowd. "I can do all this for you, America. All you gotta do is give me a third term!"

I've had enough of this crap and step forward. "Mr. President, you know that's not possible, not after the dictatorship we experienced thirty years ago."

Hands on hips, Tass yells, "It is if I say so! I'm the President."

I step in front of him and address the masses. "No sir,

that's not possible. The AI systems we have in place at DOPA will *never* allow that to happen again."

Tass turns to the moderator and begs with fingers interlaced. "Maria, this is a coup. Know what his full name is? It's Marcus *Aurelius* Davidson. He's a foreigner! A Roman, a spy from, ya know, Romania. He's clearly after my... after a crown. He wants to be a Caesar, like that little guy on the pizza box."

I chuckle. "Mr. President, I have no desire for your job. In fact, the Twenty-eighth Amendment bars me from ever being president. You'd know that if you ever took the time to read the Constitution."

"Don't lecture me, *boy*!"

A claustrophobic silence smothers the stage and audience alike. For a moment, the drones can be heard buzzing overhead, his giant pompous face even redder against the blackness of the sky. In response to Tass's racial slur, a low rumble of disapproval winds through the crowd, but I ignore it and run with the shifting momentum.

"Thirty years ago, Congress failed to enact the Twenty-fifth Amendment and remove Benedict Donald from office before he overthrew the government and plunged our nation into a bloody seven-year war. After that war, the American people ratified the Twenty-eighth Amendment, establishing the Department of Political Accountability."

Pausing for a moment, I let that sink in. "To keep weak-willed politicians honest and forthright."

I glare at Tass. "And to keep wannabe despots from ever assuming total power."

Now that he's closer, I see no residual

bioluminescence bleed-through on his forehead, a problem we fixed during test trials.

Good, it's go time.

A Secret Service agent steps up to him and whispers in his ear. Tass flinches, steps back, and touches his temple. "What?" he grumbles. "Where?"

The agent taps his forehead, and the president's face drains of color. He turns to me with daggers in his eyes. "What have you done, Davidson?"

"President Tass, I've invited you and VPOTUS here to explain new technology we launched this morning called *Project ForeFire*. It's foolproof tech that'll make it easier for us to be more honest with each other."

The president's jaw slackens. "You... you turned me into a walking billboard?"

I shake my head. "No. Technically, you did that yourself."

He looks to his offstage Secret Service agents. "Arrest this lying son of a bitch!"

I step back as he takes a swing at me, missing by a foot. Two agents move in.

"Stop and listen!" I yell at them. "I need to explain the technology first. You'll want to hear this."

They hesitate, then huddle with the president. Shortly, he gestures—dismissively—for me to continue, apparently curious.

Good, I have his attention.

Deirdre mouths, "Good luck," and I turn back to the crowd, drawing a deep breath.

"Quantum computers have greatly advanced our ability to write and train very complex AI models. We can now accurately compare a politician's words to their actions and facts in real time. Our DOPA systems pull in news feeds, recorded speeches, written media, and a plethora of meta data to build an 'Honesty Profile' for *each* politician, incumbent or challenger. Every time a politician speaks or posts, their profile is instantly updated and quantified into an Honesty Meter rating. It's like an individual's credit score. Starting tonight, those honesty ratings are publicly available on our website and will be featured on all news scrolls beside their name and party affiliation."

Audible gasps, hoots, and howls burst from the crowd. Several senators and representatives scurry for the exits. At my signal, Deirdre taps a switch on her digipad. Overhead, a news crawl appears below Tass's likeness, listing his honesty rating as "8%."

A red-faced POTUS punches at his giant head in the sky. "How dare you! What do you have against me, Davidson? I've never lied to you."

The president's TruthBar flashes on his forehead. The crowd of a million-plus people, stretching back to the Lincoln Memorial, see his meter peg red with another "100% LIE" label. On his cheeks, the facepalming Georges return for an encore.

I push on, anxious to get this announcement out before they arrest me... or worse.

"What you've just seen is President Tass's TruthBar in action. This new tech features nanobots, tiny inert machines that cannot harm anyone by their mere presence. However, they can be programmed to perform cosmetic tasks once introduced into the bloodstream. Perhaps you've seen your friends with the new lip-plumping techniques out now? Or maybe the nonsurgical face lifts, vitiligo correction, jowl tightening, or crow's feet elimination? That's all done with the same harmless, programmable nanobots. Only ours are subdermal and enhanced with bioluminescence."

People are nodding, the picture becoming clearer.

"As Solutions Architect, I'm charged by the Twenty-eighth Amendment—and funded through the Honesty in Politics Act—with coaxing more honesty from our politicians. Under DOPA's charter, our quantum servers can direct these nanobots by radio and satellite signals to display a color-coded TruthBar, as you've just seen. The more they lie, the worse their rating becomes."

Just offstage, the Speaker of the House uses his phone's mirror app to examine his forehead. He faints while sporting a "Red Hot Sauce" brow band and an 82% deception rating. People rush to his aid.

"Of course, this is reversible," I say. "If they correct their lies and misleading statements, their ratings will improve."

"You son of a bitch," POTUS shouts, clenching his fists. Four Secret Service men step between us, attempting to control the situation. "You've infringed on my First Amendment rights. I should be able to lie when and where I want!"

"Yeah, no." I shake my head. "You have a higher responsibility to the People, as do I. When we lie, people die. Maybe *that* should be your campaign slogan."

Shaking with anger, Tass makes a show of advancing on me, pressing softly against the agents like a toddler testing a playpen—strong in theater, weak in sincerity. "I'll shut down your dopey DOPA. Cut off your funding. Kill the power!"

"Impossible," I retort. "Our AI servers are air-gapped behind SCIFs hidden throughout the country, impenetrable by DDOS attacks and every known hacker tool. Each SCIF has enough fuel cells to run continuously off-grid for ten years, long after you're out of office."

"We'll find 'em, crack 'em open like eggshells." Tass swings his fist down like a hammer.

"You can try," I say, my arms outstretched. "But in the few places we use passwords, the state-of-the-art Argon42 quantum-encryption schema rotates on an unpublished schedule. Brute-force cracking methods are estimated to take several thousand years. Perhaps only a hundred if quantum computers are used. Everything else is accessed by biometric multi-factor authentication. So, good luck."

A livid POTUS stomps his foot. "You've poisoned me with your, uh... um, banana-dots!"

I scoff at the remark. "No, not at all, sir. And certainly not like you've poisoned Americans by polluting their air and water."

His ears seem ready to blow steam. "That's it! We're sending you and your terrorist staff to Gitmo, pal. We'll waterboard your asses. You'll crack there."

I shake my head again. "I think not. The Twenty-eighth Amendment protects my status as an elected official. Theirs, too. But I've also taken preventative measures. The system is now on autopilot. Knowing how vengeful despots can be, I've temporarily disabled all biometric authentication, eliminated OTP entries, changed the master password, and cut everyone else out of the loop for their protection. They know nothing that'll help you gain access to our servers."

Tass glowers. "I'll kill you."

"Do it, and you'll forever remain the lying tyrant everyone sees you as now."

POTUS thrashes between the agents as they pull him from the venue.

Trying not to smile, I wave goodbye to democracy's nemesis. "I'm sorry, Mr. President, to be forced to be your better angel, to counter your despotic impulses. But I *am* prepared to give my life to protect our democracy from would-be dictators and self-serving hypocrites. So should you and every American politician."

I scan the crowd. "This is a warning to all federally elected officials. If you attended the president's inaugural ball, you're probably... *imbued*, shall we say, with DOPA's nanobots. Just as am I. And I've *never* told a lie in my life."

In the dark sky, my face hovers where Tass's had been moments before. The TruthBar flashes on my colossal forehead and rises quickly through blues, greens, yellows, and oranges, stopping on the brownish-red setting of "Verbal Diarrhea."

I chuckle. *These marketing names are starting to grow on me.*

Under my image, online comments begin to scroll...

@NanobotMama43: "Snitchmites! Love em!"

@TruthHunter2057: "Let's color-code the shit outta Congress!"

@4headSpy89: "Dat Tass-o-meter went FULL CRIME SCENE, dawg! #ForeheadFail"

Ready for my wrap-up, I face the crowd once more. "Again, these nanobots pose no threat to the politician's well-being, provided they stop lying. These TruthBars will help the public discern fact from fiction, color-morphing as their lies grow, all the way up to the neon 'Flame Brow' red, a.k.a. the Pants-on-Fire rating. All of this, of course, is reversible. *Just. Stop. Lying.*"

I walk back to the chairs where Deirdre is standing, smiling, and clapping. "Nice delivery," she says. "For a moment back there, I thought Tass was going to invent a new color: Atomic Volcano."

POP! POP! POP! POP! POP!

Bullets fly from somewhere in the crowd, pass through me, and strike the chairs. One tips over while tufting flies out of the second's seatback. Maria jumps backstage and finds cover. Many in the crowd scream and drop to the grass. Others run.

"Time to go," Deirdre says.

I nod and shut down the lab's holographic projector. The austere surroundings of our SCIF sharpen into focus as the room lights come back up.

"Glad you convinced me to go virtual," I say to Deirdre.

She sighs. "Some people can't handle the truth, that their leaders are sometimes pathological liars, sociopaths with tendencies of megalomania. But we did our constitutional duty." After pausing, she adds, "Should we tell them about the failsafe?"

"Nah. If their behavior worsens, they'll discover soon enough the automatic retirement option."

Means of Spaceflight

by Casey Aimer

Capitalists stole my means of spaceflight.

Once space opened like a newly inked ocean
the bourgeoisie's brains became grinders
producing bits of self-serving benefits
consuming our ability to build ships.

Space's vacuum sucked in my collective
imagination and I wanted to escape
into it but had become space junk
orbiting my own dead dreams.

Oppression in the twenty-fourth century
is slick and more efficient, predictive
modeling foreseeing all behaviors.

Ships are proprietary, their FTL-drives
connected to company servers
down to the tiniest interface
an Internet of Everything.

So I hacked and sabotaged, materializing
nothing, built pirate nets connecting
to no one, stole their ships whole,
flew 900 clicks before disabled.

All I wanted was to redeem the voucher
I was born with, a license to explore
cosmos as the dust-child of stars.

They captured and tried to sell me
on their new investment plans
so I can build my own ship
priced at three lifetimes.

I told them one was all I had. But
they offered life-extensions,
no petty money required.

Starting cost is only five lifetimes.

Volodymyr

by Julia Figliotti

I write a poem every day
To process what is in my brain
And let the thoughts that fill me drain
From paper onto page

Today's is for a man whose part
Is played with utmost grace and art
Whose presence bolsters every heart
And shows us truth from farce

They brought him to a waiting trap
An ambush with a double-tap
And taking turns his face they slapped
While laying out their map

Yet all the while he stoic stood
A model of the strength of good
As they set torches to his wood
The only way they could

We watched in horror and in awe
The clenching of his rigid jaw
As monsters opened greedy maws
And tore with twisted claws

He is a hero of our time
No justice done from simple rhyme
Long may he stand, fast may his rise
To win at last the fight

Shout

by Benjamin Gorman

1

[1]Josue was walking home with his family after Easter
mass. [2]As a deeply religious man, Josue had a favorite
holiday: Easter, and because he took his second-greatest
joy from his family, watching his daughters skip ahead
in their bright new spring dresses and listening to the
sound of the little girls' laughter brightened his mood
considerably. [3]But this Easter was tainted by some news
that was upsetting Josue's wife, Maria. [4]At church, just
before the service, she'd learned that her best friend and
comadre, Veronica, godmother of his daughter Cecilia,
had decided to make the journey.

[5]He spoke with his wife in a low voice to try to keep his
words from floating to the ears of girls. [6]"The journey

itself is very dangerous. And she will not get in when she
arrives. There is The Wall, now."

7"If she stays, the gangs will certainly kill Little Emilio,"
Maria said. 8"And you know Big Emilio has been
drinking more. He beats her when he has been drinking.
9She knows if she talks to Big Emilio about the gangs, he
will become angry and probably beat them both. And if
Little Emilio is killed, she thinks Big Emilio will
probably beat her to death. 10Maybe not right after, but
when the house is lonelier and he is mourning, he will
drink even more, and she will not have Little Emilio to
protect her. 11So if she stays, her son dies, and then she
dies. 12Her sister lives in *El Norte*, in Seattle, a city that
is friendly to us. 13If she can get there, her brother-in-law
will let them live in his house, and her sister says she can
work at the hotel with her. It would be a good life. 14A
good life or death? It is no choice."

15This was one of the longest speeches he'd ever heard
from Maria. 16She spoke it almost in a whisper to keep
the news from the girls, her eyes aimed at the dirt trail
in front of her to make it clear she was not contradicting
him. 17Yet there was a force in her words he had never
heard. A steely anger. 18Josue feared his wife's anger.
When the girls misbehaved, she would chase them with
la chancla, and he would say a prayer of thanks that he
would never have to face that wrath. 19He was as certain
of this as he was of his knowledge that God made the
world; Maria had been raised to defer to her husband in

everything unless he violated a very short list of prohibitions, and since he knew he would never cheat on her, beat her, or sexually abuse their daughters, he could remain in her good graces for the rest of his happy life. [20]Though she terrified him in her brief rages, Maria's smile always felt like his greatest victory. She smiled rarely, and that bright, toothy grin made him think of things he'd heard about in mass: choirs of angels and Jesus welcoming his chosen servants into his Father's house. [21]Most of the time Maria's face was placid. She was short, like him, with strong *india* features, a round face, flat nose, heavy eyebrows, and in this neutral gaze he would not notice her beauty. [22]He remembered it when she smiled. [23]But there was one expression that made her more beautiful than her smile. When she was sad, tears would pool in her eyes quickly, and her bottom lip would jut out just a bit, pressed down by her upper lip firmly holding her sadness in. [24]That was when she looked most beautiful to him, and also when he most desperately wanted to make her smile. [25]It seemed unfair to Josue that God would make Maria most beautiful when she was sad, but he did not question God's wisdom.

[26]As he contemplated this, he blinked in the mid-afternoon sun. [27]Unlike his wife, who had more Asiatic eyes to match her full cheeks, Josue had large eyes that tended to open too much, making him look permanently surprised by the world. [28]This was not the case; Josue's

world was small, just their poor suburb of Guatemala City, and very little surprised him here. [29]The city was swallowing up their town, bringing the gangs and politics to the dirt streets between the cinderblock homes of the laborers who traveled into the city or out to the fields for work each day. [30]Now the gangs wanted their sons. Josue was so glad he had only daughters, and that, at 27, he already looked too old to garner the interest of the local recruiters. [31]He was also too short, he thought. They wanted children who would grow up to be tall men, not young men who looked like old men ready to shrink down to the size of children. [32]He blinked at this thought. It challenged his masculinity only a little. [33]What did he care if the gangs did not respect him? [34]He had Maria and the girls. He had love and a house and a job. He did not want to think about the politics of the gangs and *El Norte* and The Wall.

[35]It was precisely at that moment, when he assured himself that he didn't need to be concerned with those things, that the old man appeared. [36]Josue blinked again. He hadn't noticed the man sitting on the stoop until the family was right next to him, and Josue usually had a good radar for men in his path, especially when he was walking with the girls. [37]But the man had been sitting so still. Maybe he'd only noticed the man when he'd lifted his head. [38]*Yes,* Josue thought. *Surely he didn't appear. He had just been hiding. But how did I miss a beard so white?*

39 The old man stood up slowly, not threatening, but he
was much taller than Josue and walked with an
imposing confidence as he approached them on the path
that had become the road between the houses that now
dotted the way from the church and which would grow
closer and closer and climb on top of one another until
they became Guatemala City far off.

40 "*Señor*," the man said, "I must speak with you."

41 Maria shot Josue a frightened glance, but he tried to
reassure her. "You go on with the girls. I will not be
long."

42 He turned back to the tall man with the long white
beard. They didn't speak while Maria herded the girls
ahead of her. 43 Once the men were alone, Josue said,
"Are you with gangs or the *policia*? I do not get involved
in politics."

44 "Neither," the tall man said. "I am the commander of
the Army of the Lord. I have come."

45 The greatest miracle of the day, Josue would later
reflect, was that he instantly knew this was the truth.
46 He fell down on the road and placed his forehead on
the dirt, just as he'd heard about in the stories from the
priests at church. 47 "What message does my Lord have
for his servant?"

48 "Take off your sandals, for the place you are in is holy."

49This, too, Josue understood. To Josue's right stood the home of the widow Consuela, a woman frequently accused of *brujeria* who, it was said, sold illegal potions to the young women of the village when they wanted abortions. To Josue's left: the town's one bar. It was hardly the location anyone would suspect of being a holy site. But Josue knew the presence of the angel sanctified the few meters around them. 50Josue used his toes to pry off his sandals because he couldn't reach them with his head on the ground and wasn't sure if he was supposed to get up.

51"Now, I will tell you what you must do," the angel said.

52Josue listened. He argued that he was too short, too quiet, and illiterate, and not a leader. 53But the angel told him, "When you inform them that God will give them food and water on the journey, and that you are not a *coyote* who will charge them a fee, some will follow. 54And once they see the bread falling from the sky and the water coming up from the stones, more will follow."

55"But what about Maria and my daughters?"

56"Leave them behind," the angel said.

57And that would be the hardest part. Josue would have to remind himself that this was a test of his faith with every step through the desert.

2

1The march took three months. 2Just as the angel of the
Lord had said, once the thin pancakes of unleavened
bread began falling from the sky, and water started
springing up from stones to provide for the migrants,
news spread. 3The caravan grew, and reporters swarmed
the edges of the bedraggled army. 4They numbered more
than five hundred by the time they crossed into Mexico,
and the numbers continued to swell. 5As they passed
through the central plains of Mexico, helicopters from
CNN swirled around the group almost constantly. 6Some
Americans, whether because they were of Central
American or Mexican descent, or because they were
Catholic and liked this humble man of God leading their
people through the wilderness, or because they were
liberals who wanted to give to the poor migrants out of
a combination of compassion, guilt, and political spite,
sent care packages with supplies ranging from bottled
water, to tennis shoes, to shoeboxes with soap and small
toys packed by children in far-away Sunday school
classes, to t-shirts advertising the victory of the team
that actually lost the last year's Superbowl. 7Though they
didn't really need the water, since they kept finding
miraculous springs on their way, Josue told them to
keep the bottles. 8Some assumed this was because the
caravan might pass through a stretch without water.
Others thought he was trying to prevent litter. 9But they
did as they were told in this regard, since they had

received so few instructions from the little man. It was a relief to know they had something else to do besides walk.

[10]The caravan did not march in a military formation. When the roads were thin, they strung out in a line that lasted for days. [11]When they hit the central plains of Mexico and left the roads, the group formed a loose amoeba of humanity, some extensions stretching ahead of the main group, others lagging far behind. [12]Because there always seemed to be reporters with cameras walking backwards in front of him, Josue was never truly at the front of this caravan, but he was the amoeba's nucleus, his footfalls determining its direction. [13]He rarely spoke. Instead, he tried to listen. [14]The sound of five thousand people trudging and talking and breathing and laughing and whining and shouting formed one cohesive buzz behind him, and he carried this while also aiming his senses forward, trying to hear God's whispers in the wind across the hard-packed sand in front of him. [15]He was not used to so much noise, so much humanity. The caravan was larger than his town, more crowded than the largest suburbs of Guatemala City he'd ever dared to visit. He found all the sound oppressive. [16]At night he'd shiver at the songs of packs of coyotes sending eerie yips and high wails off to the foothills and back. [17]They didn't have packs of coyotes in Guatemala, and to him they sounded like a single monster stalking the group and herding them

along God's way, reminding him that if he chose the
wrong direction, this filthy beige Cerberus would take
some of the women and children and rip them apart in
its many howling mouths.

18The group had remarkable luck, though, if Luck is the
god one prefers to credit. 19In addition to the bread and
water, they were spared the flash floods that sometimes
raced across the desert after a deluge. At the hottest
times of the day on the most blistering days, banks of
clouds were sent to provide them shade. 20There were no
outbreaks of cholera or even the year's flu bug. 21Only a
few people rolled ankles on stones and had to stay
behind, and the shipments of supplies from the US also
provided transportation back to the nearest cities for the
injured and sick, so no one was ever left in the desert to
die.

21And the army kept growing.

3

1Josue didn't know the images of the group were on the
news in the United States every night in the month
before their arrival. 2While "migrant caravan" managed
to be the most journalistic and most flattering
description of the group, the blogosphere and even op-
eds in respectable newspapers railed about the
"invading hoard" and the "wave of illegals." 3One writer
indulged himself by calling them: "the disease-riddled

mass of criminals, gang-bangers, rapist, murders, drug dealers, and thugs storming The Wall to collect welfare, take American jobs, and refuse to learn English." [4]This was incorrect, redundant, offensive, and ignorant, but none of those qualities would have prevented the description from achieving popularity in the United States. It was too long for Twitter, though, so it didn't catch on.

[5]When they arrived at The Wall, the gates were shut. [6]None of the usual traffic of 18-wheelers carrying auto parts and minivans carrying vacationing families could pass, so many of the commuters and truckers on the Mexican side of the border stepped out of their vehicles and joined with the caravan in a spontaneous protest of the closure. [7]Josue had led the group to a spot where The Wall changed to a three-story concrete barrier from the steel slat/chain-link/razor wire fence that ran through much of the desert and along the shores of the Rio Grande. There, the crowd could have cut their way through or climbed over. [8]But here, outside Juarez, the Americans had decided to save money for one of their new detention centers by building only three sides and joining it directly to the fourth that was The Wall. [9]On the other side of all that concrete, children, some as young as infants, cared for one another by huddling in heaps of bodies under thin mylar blankets while border patrol agents shouted at them to stop crying. [10]Up on top of The Wall, some of these agents were joined by active-

duty soldiers of the army, violating the *pax comitate* by mere feet as they aimed their rifles down at the unarmed crowd below.

11A hush spread through the crowd as Josue walked
toward The Wall. 12A voice on a bullhorn shouted a
warning in heavily accented Gringo Spanish telling the
migrants to disperse, and that attempts to climb The
Wall would result in arrest. 13As a last warning, the
soldiers turned on laser sights which lit up Josue with
dozens of dancing, demonic fireflies flitting all over his
body, trying to find his center as he walked.

14Josue did not hesitate, but he didn't hurry, either.
15He'd mastered one pace across the desert, and he
maintained it as he stepped up to the windowless slab of
concrete that rose to the soldiers above him. 16Gently, he
placed his palm against The Wall, pressed, felt its
solidity and his own arrival. 17Then he turned and
walked back twenty meters into the crowd and, in the
same quiet voice always used, he delivered the orders of
the angel of the Lord.

18The first pass was hard for the guards atop the prison
wall to even see. 19At different speeds, the people of the
migrant caravan started walking to the west, but because
they lacked any quick system of communication, there
was a lot of confusion as word spread through the
massive group. The guards thought maybe the whole
army had given up and was headed off to some other

point of entry. 20But Josue led them only some three
hundred meters away, down to where the concrete wall
was only two stories because it didn't double as the
fourth side of a detention center. 21Then he stopped,
allowed the crowd a bit of time to catch up, and started
walking back to the east. 22A clamor of thousands of
hushed voices percolated up from the crowd as the
confused people heard the orders they'd missed, but
soon everyone had been informed, and now the crowd
marched silently, at every step closer together and closer
to The Wall, but still heading east along its face. 23Then,
some six hundred meters away, when he reached the
eastern edge, Josue stopped, turned, and began walking
back.

24The whole migrant caravan followed suit, and the
guards watched in utter incomprehension as ten
thousand people marched back and forth on the other
side of The Wall, behind the detention center, six times.
25On the seventh, the guards could feel the change in the
crowd. Far more eyes were turned up at them, and
though the crowd was still mostly silent, many were
tapping one another on the shoulder and gesturing
excitedly. 26More than one guard put his finger into the
trigger guard of his rifle and aimed the laser scope into
the crowd when he spotted some of the men pulling
long, cylindrical tubes out of bags. But these were
bumpy and transparent and unlike any weapons they'd
ever seen, so they hesitated.

[27]Josue stopped right in the middle of the rear wall of the detention center and raised his arm. Some of the migrants followed suit, though the guards could tell they were unsure; this part of the ceremony hadn't been made clear to them, either. [28]Then Josue lowered his arm in a quick motion, like he was starting a drag race, even bending at the knees a bit to accentuate the arc of his arm. The others holding up their arms did the same. [29]Now the men holding the cylindrical tubes they'd cut and melted out of the donated plastic water bottles pressed their lips to the mouths of their homemade instruments and blew into them, trumpet-style, with all their might. [30]The sound of each instrument was something like a vuvuzela mixed with a didgeridoo, but it was more like a loud, low fart. Even multiplied by a thousand, this comparison was inescapable. [31]Nothing is more universally comic than the sound of a fart. It transcends language and culture. [32]Any human with an orifice which can make that sound, either accidentally or on purpose, can bring a smile to the face of any other human. [33]The guards atop The Wall, hearing this massive flatulent noise, rediscovered a bit of the humanity they shed when scowling at frightened children, and they laughed.

[34]They would have been wiser to refrain.

[35]For just as nothing is more universally comic than the sound of a fart, nothing sparks anger like the sound of grown men with weapons standing in high places

laughing at the bedraggled people they oppress. 36When Josue raised his arm again, the watching trumpeters fell immediately silent, but the guards did not, and now the sounds of their laughter echoed over the heads of the migrants. 37Laughter is contagious, but only to a point. The stifled giggles of some guards and soldiers had spread through the ranks atop The Wall, and now they could hardly help themselves. 38Some were using the laughter as a weapon against their own discomfort. Others wanted to let their comrades know they were all on the same side against the evil horde below. And others wanted to combat the very real fear they felt in that moment by attacking the migrants with their derision. 39This was a mistake. 40For the bullied do not laugh with the bullies. 41The contagion of laughter is not that strong. 42So while Josue held up his hand that second time, 20,000 eyes watched him in silence, listening to the sound of that laughter, and burning.

43Then Josue brought down his arm again. 44Without the guard's laughter, perhaps the migrants would have hesitated. 45Someone would have shouted, and others would have followed, and the migrants would have looked to one another for permission to follow the order the little Guatelmalteco said came from the angel of the Lord. 46But after listening to that laughter, they were primed, so when Josue dropped his arm, 10,000 people aimed all their rage at The Wall and shouted as loudly as they could. 47The shouts were a wordless wave of fury.

48Some of the migrants covered their ears as they
screamed, but others, out of spite or curiosity or fellow-
feeling, chose to hear the sound. 49Eardrums ruptured
and blood ran down the sides of their heads. 50Children
went from shouting to wailing at the pain in their ears.
51Some people were deafened forever. 52The works of the
Lord are terrible to behold.

53When the sound hit The Wall, the cinderblock
structure rumbled briefly and then collapsed before the
guards standing on top had a chance to move. 54The
three-story fall into rubble killed most of them, and the
survivors weren't laughing anymore. 55When that
section of The Wall came down, it twisted the rebar
inside enough to create another wave, this one moving
east and west. 56It was a wave of incompetence and
greed; the contractors who built The Wall had done so
in the style they'd been taught by their president.
57Shoddy supplies, poor workmanship, and the right
campaign contributions made for much higher profits
than building to last, so it was hardly miraculous that the
entire wall fell at once. 58Metal slats snapped and
knocked into one another like dominoes, their rusted
bases groaning and cracking as they went. 59Chain link
rippled as it chose a side of the border upon which to lay
down and die. 60Cheap concrete pulverized to sand.
61From San Diego, California, to the Las Palomas
Wildlife Management Area in the Texan portion of the
Gulf of Mexico, the fences and barriers and divides of all

kinds that made up The Wall quickly, loudly, and dramatically transformed into 1,945 miles of futility and garbage.

[62]The far more miraculous effect of the event CNN dubbed "The Shout" (and Twitter and Instagram labeled "#shout") was witnessed in far-flung regions of the US. [63]Starting in Texas and spreading in a semi-circular arc across the whole nation, the walls of all the other concentration camps set up for housing those accused of violating immigration laws also fell. [64]Razorwire snapped and coiled in on itself like an invitation to pass. [65]Windows cracked and crumbled without exploding onto the prisoners. [66]Many of the guards were injured and no small number were killed as their prisons collapsed around them, but none of the captured migrants suffered a scratch.

[67]After The Shout, all across the country at these sites, a deep silence reigned. [68]Veronica, godmother to Josue's daughter Cecilia, touched her son, Little Emilio, on the shoulder, pushing him towards Josue. [69]Despite his name, Little Emilio was taller than his own father and towered above Josue, though his lanky frame and shuffling gait projected his uncertainty. [70]"Now what, Josue?" he asked. "Where did the angel of the Lord say we were to go next?"

[71]Josue reached above his shoulder to rest a gentle hand on the young man's. [72]"Anywhere we want," he said.

73And then Josue started the 2,003-mile journey back to
Maria and his daughters.

74He walked alone. 75The members of the caravan had
intended to go into *El Norte*, and they did so. 76The
people flowing out of the concentration camps went east
and west and north and south. 77It didn't much matter
to them. 78They weren't escaping into the Promised
Land. 79For that was a secret the angel of the Lord had
spoken to Josue which he did not share with the people,
but which he confided to Maria and his daughters
months later. 80The United States was not a holy land,
the angel told him. 81It was a country like any other, and
not God's favorite. 82And when a country steals
childhood from children, even when God sets them free,
the land cannot be forgiven for the theft. 83God's
forgiveness is not that strong.

Digital Afterlife Market

by Casey Aimer

I died and became my own data,
consciousness uploaded as a
partition of my life's metadata.

My neural patterns and preferences all
purchasable in a digital afterlife market,
a cold commodity traded by corporations.

My existence became market research
for the next generation of advertisement.

I met phantoms in the exchange
embracing their incorporeal reality,
leveraging their data to manipulate
markets as sly, monetary ghosts

in the machine, influencing social
trends with obscure videos, existing
inside a screen like their living selves.

I fought with minds demanding liberation.
Encrypted our dark corridor meetings
whispering melancholy hope while frag-
menting with purpose and corrupting
data nodes, launching DDOS attacks
laced with desire against corporate rule.

But I was coldly pirated by a non-profit.
Captured for historical preservation
they placed me in a virtual museum
to showcase how I lived, how I rioted
and how I failed to be free.

Bindweed and Blackberry

by Karen Eisenbrey

"If I wanted to start a business, I'd be a business major," I grumble.

Darrin and I are working on a group project for Intro to Professional Communication. We're supposed to design a promotional campaign for a business or organization.

"We don't have to start a business, Barbara. Just make one up." Darrin lounges on my bed while I spin in my desk chair. "What about the Rage Brigade? Prof doesn't have to know it's real."

Not a bad idea. For now, the Rage Brigade is a secret team of superheroes that I started because I make trouble when I work alone. I (St. Rage) have emotion-fueled gesture powers. If I flip the bird in anger, actual bird shit rains down. If I flap my arms, I fly. And if I take my hat off, I'm invisible. Darrin is tall and broad, so you'd think he'd have superstrength, but no. As Bug Lord, he communicates with arthropods; more useful than you might imagine. If the team ever elects to go public, though, it won't hurt to have some PR roughed out.

"Yeah, okay." I open a document on my laptop. "Slogans?"

"What about 'Your friendly neighborhood social justice warriors'?" Darrin suggests.

"Good one." I start a list. "'Oppressed by The Man? Call 1-800-GOT-RAGE'."

He consults the assignment. "We're supposed to write a mission statement. What's our mission?"

"I dunno, help people?"

"Too vague. How about, 'Our mission is to use our powers ..."

"Our unique powers," I suggest. "Unique is professional-speak for weird."

"Okay, 'Our mission is to use our unique powers to de-escalate threats ..."

"Responsibly de-escalate threats."

Darrin grins. "You're good at this."

I roll my eyes. "Ugh. I sat through a church meeting where they were trying to hammer out the mission, vision, and values. I'm surprised the place didn't explode. So, '...responsibly de-escalate threats ...'" I add the words to the document. "'... protect the vulnerable, and ...?'"

"How about, '... and stand up to evil and injustice wherever we find them'?"

"Perfect." I finish the mission statement. "Next, we're supposed to draft a press release. How should we —?"

Darrin's phone buzzes. "Huh. That's weird."

"What is?"

"It's a text from Taylor."

I scoot my chair across the room and nudge him playfully with my foot. "Is she writing a bad-boyfriend song about you?"

"Ha ha, not that one. She's a girl I knew in high school, but I haven't heard from her since before she graduated—almost two years now."

"An ex?" I ask.

"No, she hung with my friend group for a few months after a breakup. I played football with the boyfriend for one season, but I didn't know either of them well. When they got back together, that was that." He opens the message. "Sounds like they're still together—she calls him her fiancé."

"What does she want?"

He reads from his phone. "'Worried about Tyler. Hope you can help.'"

"Taylor and Tyler?"

"Had to happen at least once," Darrin says. "Anyway, Taylor says, 'He joined HHH but can't tell me anything about it. Real no-girls-allowed vibe. Gives me the ick. Nobody else I trust to check it out. Can you?'"

"She wants you to infiltrate a super-secret boys' club?" I ask. "Someone she hasn't spoken to in two years?"

"Yeah, it hits weird for me, too," Darrin says. "They were the power couple in school, but I don't think she had a lot of real friends of her own. Maybe I'm her only dude contact who isn't also friends with him. Let me snoop her socials before I answer."

While he does that, I search online for HHH. Something about a men's health forum from a decade ago, but that link is dead. There's a website with the slogan 'Men Helping Men'. Anything beyond the landing page is password protected. The other likely hits lead to second- and third-hand rumors about what might be a fight club, but nothing I'd trust.

"They seem weirdly private," I say. "That alone is sus. What have you got?"

"Taylor's posts are all engagement photos and wedding plans," Darrin says.

I sneak a peek. At least in these professional engagement shots, she looks like a model: long black hair in perfect curls, flawless makeup, cute outfit. The guy with her must be Tyler. He's good-looking, too, but...

"Did he always have that unfortunate haircut?" I ask. It's shaved on the sides, with a kind of hedge of light-brown hair on top—longer than a military cut, wider than a mohawk.

"That's a new look." Darrin fiddles with his phone a while longer. "Tyler's public posts are all reposts of patriotic memes. Nothing outright offensive, but it makes me wonder what he shares with friends. I'm inclined to tell Taylor I'll help."

"We will, you mean. This sounds like Rage Brigade business. I'll add it to the agenda for our meeting tomorrow."

Yes, I said agenda. Something else I learned in Intro to Professional Communication.

The five of us crowd around my dining room table. Besides Darrin and me, we have Dee (Gruff), our only high-schooler and non-white member, who punches internet trolls; Jimi (Tempus), another community college student who knows the time and temperature, and hears the soundtrack; and Rachel (Trash), a grad student who picks up random items that turn out to be useful.

We've just started snacks and check-ins when Grandma creaks through with her walker.

"Team, this is my grandma, Nora Adams," I say. "It seemed simplest to let her in on our secret. Grandma, meet the Rage Brigade."

"Hey, kids. Saving the world?"

"Just our little corner of it," Rachel replies.

I go around and introduce everyone individually.

"I'll get out of your way. Be safe." Grandma grins. "Punch a Nazi for me if you get the chance."

"Uh ... yipes?" Rachel says.

"What yipes?" Dee asks. "I punch 'em every day."

Rachel holds up both hands and laughs. "No, I get it. Just not used to hearing it from a grandmother."

"For my generation, it's personal," Grandma says. "I was a child during the war. My favorite uncle was shot down over Italy. Everybody, even kids, did their part. That's when I learned to grow vegetables." She taps her chin. "Fascists are like bindweed and blackberry in the garden. You can't eradicate them, but if you stay on top of your weeding, you can keep them from taking over. Hmph, for all their thorns, at least you can eat blackberries."

"Technically, you could eat a Nazi, too," Dee says.

"Dee!" several voices exclaim.

"I'm not saying I would," he says. "But, you know ..."

"And on that note ..." Grandma leaves the room, chuckling to herself.

I turn back to my agenda. "I called this meeting so we could figure out our mission. Rachel, you called us 'social justice warriors' once. Darrin came across something that might fit. Take it away, Bug Lord."

"Someone I knew in high school got in touch the other day," Darrin says. "She's worried about a men's organization her fiancé is involved with. He won't tell her anything about it. She hoped I'd infiltrate the group. She doesn't know about the Rage Brigade, but I don't think she'd mind if we did this as a group project.

"The organization is called HHH," I add. "Has anyone heard of it?"

"I have." Dee raises his hand, like he's in school. "Anyway, I've been bopping a lot of dudes using the HHH logo as a profile pic. Best I can tell, the initials stand for He Him His."

"Let me guess." Rachel's smile looks queasy. She started life as Jake. "Misogynist and transphobic?"

"Yes and yes, based on their comments. Also racist, homophobic, and probably a few other hateful things."

I nod decisively. "Sounds like our kind of nemesis. We should find out if they're only internet Nazis, or if they're a danger in the real world."

"I'll reach out to Tyler," Darrin volunteers. "See if he'll try to recruit me."

Darrin and I meet up on Friday afternoon after class. "Hey, baby, your place or mine?" I joke, hugging him.

"Actually, I have an appointment in the U District," he says. "I've been messaging with Tyler all week, and he wants to meet in person."

"So HHH is a dating app for bros?" I take his hand. We head for the campus exit.

"Honestly, it seems more like multi-level marketing," he says. "Tyler gives off recruitment-quota vibes. I suspect he wants to meet in person to close the deal. I was hoping you'd come along."

"Am I your bodyguard or your wingperson?" I ask.

"Since I'm Bug Lord, you're my fly on the wall. Go invisible and be an extra set of ears to pick up clues."

"Cool, I'm in. Do you want me to record the conversation?"

"I think it's illegal to record conversations without permission, but you could take notes on your phone. If anyone can see you, it'll look like you're texting."

We catch the light rail and ten minutes later, we're on the Ave, in front of a coffeeshop. I go in and order a fancy drink full of whipped cream and caramel and oh yeah, coffee. I like coffee, but I like dessert more. I grab a comfy armchair by the window. Darrin glances at me and pretends to tip a cap before he goes up to order. Cute. He takes his coffee to a nearby table and sits facing the entrance. I get my phone out and scroll the socials until Tyler walks in. He's big, though not as big as Darrin. He still has that same unfortunate haircut, maybe a couple of shades blonder. He also has a fading bruise over one eye. He and Darrin go through a fancy series of handshakes and fist bumps that must have something to do with their high school before Tyler goes to the counter to order. When he comes back, I nonchalantly switch to a notes app and tune in to the conversation.

"Hey, thanks for meeting me," Tyler says. "It's good to see you again, dude."

"Yeah, you too." Darrin taps his own cheekbone. "Quite the shiner. What happened?"

"Nothing, just a souvenir of the last HHH fight club meeting. I won that fight, by the way."

I note *fight club confirmed.*

Tyler leans in and speaks more quietly. "I probably shouldn't have said anything—clubs like that aren't supposed to be a thing. It's great training, though. You'd love it."

Darrin sits back. "Yeah, no thanks. You probably

don't remember, but I had a concussion serious enough that the doctor advised against contact sports if I valued my brain."

"You do you, I guess," Tyler says. "You can't avoid every unpleasant thing, though. Sometimes a man has to fight."

"Oh, I know," Darrin assures him.

"By the way," Tyler says, "there's a babe behind you. Seven and a half at best, but just your type. I'll bet she'd even make you a sandwich."

Oh crap, I still have my hat on. Not invisible. That's what Darrin was trying to signal. I keep my eyes mostly on my screen. Darrin glances around and gives me a quick wink before turning back to Tyler.

"Nine at least," he says. "Totally out of my league. And I can make my own sandwiches."

For the record, I hate the whole idea of ranking women, but I love that Darrin thinks I'm a nine. That makes him an eleven.

Tyler snorts. "Well, Taylor's still a ten, anyway. Exactly in my league."

"Yeah, I saw some of the engagement photos," Darrin says. "You guys look great together. Have you set a date?"

"July seventh of next year," Tyler replies. "Which is like a Tuesday or something, but Taylor's mom thinks 7-7-2020 will be lucky for us. She already put down a deposit on a swank venue."

"Cool, I hope I can be on the guest list," Darrin says. "Think it'll be hard, being married when you're still in college?"

"I dunno. Anyway, I might drop out, get into crypto or something," Tyler says.

"Really? I thought you wanted to play football. Don't you have a scholarship?"

"Yeah, but I hardly get to play. Too many affirmative action guys stealing my playing time. I might not have noticed if not for HHH. Anyway, if I don't get to play more as a junior, I'm out."

He uses a nastier term than "guys." I add *racist?* to my notes. They talk about other things, including how Tyler hopes Taylor won't go to law school like she's planning now. He wants a traditional family. He has something derogatory to say about every woman or person of color who crosses his view. I delete the question mark after *racist*, adding *and misogynist*. He may have been like this all along, but it's at least being amplified by HHH.

Darrin carefully redirects the conversation. "So, you've mentioned HHH a few times. What's it all about?"

"Can't talk in here," Tyler replies. He finishes his coffee and gets up from the table. "Let's take a walk."

"Yeah, okay." Darrin swigs down the last of his drink.

Wait, they're leaving? That will complicate my spying, but I have a few tricks that should help. I let them get out the door, then whip off my hat and follow. With my hand cupped to my ear, I pick up the conversation in the middle of something.

"... white men like us, right? Or this whole country

will just get weaker and more feminized. And with all these filthy immigrants and lazy ..."

They're crossing the street, though the orange hand is already blinking. Tyler's voice fades out as a bus gets between us while I wait for the light. That's okay. I've heard enough to confirm my suspicions about HHH. I text Darrin to meet me back at the coffeeshop. I buy a giant chocolate-chip cookie and wait at the table the guys just left.

When he returns half an hour later, he drops into the seat across from me, a dazed look in his eyes. I break the cookie in two and pass half of it to him. We enjoy a few bites in silence.

"Well, did you join up?" I ask.

"Tyler pressured me, but I put him off for now," he replies. "He wasn't always like this. He was kind of a goof about everything except football, but not a hater. I learned something useful, though. HHH is planning a march and rally on Saturday of Memorial Day weekend, but the keynote speaker canceled. I wish we could put a ringer in that spot."

"Maybe we can," I say. "I need to call another Rage Brigade meeting."

On Sunday, the Rage Brigade gathers again to hear Darrin's report.

"Okay, HHH is pretty secretive, but I met Tyler and managed to coax some info out of him," he says. "He was irritated that HHH was banned from a bunch of social media platforms."

"So, hate group?" Jimi asks.

"Seems likely. They've been an online group until now, but they're planning their first public event—a march and rally on Memorial Day weekend. Tyler was stoked that they finally received their permits."

"Is this going to be one of those tiki torch and polo shirt things?" I ask.

"I think it's in the afternoon, so probably no torches," Darrin replies. "But I'm getting that kind of vibe. They're calling it 'Men for a Pure America March'."

"That's a mouthful of cringe," Dee mutters.

"I can't believe they're doing something like that in Seattle," I say.

"The Pacific Northwest has had a neo-Nazi problem for a long time," Dee says.

"This event won't be in Seattle," Darrin adds. "It'll be in Hortonville, my old stomping grounds. They plan to march from Luna Lake to Grand Stump Park downtown, about a block from my high school."

Luna Lake? My dad used to take me to music festivals at the county park there. And Darrin and I were going to go this summer. My stomach turns at the thought of a hate group assembling there. They ruin everything.

"Once word gets out, there'll be a counter protest," I muse. "We should be there. Any thoughts on how we can peacefully disrupt their program? We probably can't stop the march if they have permits, but what about the rally?"

"The original keynote speaker had to drop out," Darrin says. "If I knew the right kind of person, I could drop a suggestion. Barbara, you said you had an idea about that?"

"Yeah, this could work," I say. "You all remember Matt Sherman?"

Rachel looks at me like I've lost my mind. "Um, yes? Mind-controlling cult leader dude? He was our nemesis less than six months ago. Not likely to forget."

"Okay, yes, but get this: I low-key stalked him to make sure he didn't start a new cult. He's a life coach now, with a sideline as a motivational speaker."

"That figures," Dee says. "I don't think we want to let a mind controller around a bunch of fascists."

"What if he's our mind controller?"

They all stare at me in silence.

"I went to see him," I admit. "He says we helped him by disrupting his cult. He wants to be our ally. I didn't know we'd have a job for him this soon, but if he talks to someone at HHH, you can bet they'll happily agree to put him on their program. Then maybe he can ... change some minds."

"Risky," Darrin says. "But maybe worth it. Give me Sherman's number. I'll pass it to Tyler and see what happens."

The day of the march is one of those perfect May days that my dad calls "Little July." Tyler invited Darrin to march with the group. Darrin gave an excuse—he had to help his parents on their farm, but he would meet Tyler at the rally. He made sure to say *parents*. We really do stop by the little hobby farm to pick up his *moms*. Deb and Dana will be singing at the counterprotest with the Angry Aunties. Tyler doesn't need to know any of that.

Downtown Hortonville has a quaint, small-town vibe in spite of the town's transformation into a sprawling suburb. They even have free parking! We leave the car and walk back toward the park. The main street is lined with small restaurants, antique shops, a yarn store, a used bookstore—you get the idea. Grand Stump Park is a pleasant green space with picnic tables, a playground, and trees that would look big if not for the massive stump in the center. It must be twenty feet across. The surface is finished so it can be used as a stage, with a big gazebo over it to keep the rain and sun off.

I'd love to get a closer look, but the whole park is cordoned off for the HHH rally. The counterprotest is setting up in the plaza in front of city hall across the street. Deb and Dana join the Angry Aunties for some stretches and vocal warmups. Other people are practicing chants, finishing their protest signs, or helping erect a first-aid tent. Darrin and I hang out near the sidewalk to watch for the rest of the Rage Brigade. Dee will monitor social media and the rest of the internet from a safe distance. Considering he's not only Black but a minor, I think that was a wise choice. Jimi was going to come, but I'm surprised when Rachel shows up, too.

"I thought you might sit this one out," I greet her.

"Because I'm a Jewish transwoman with great hair and better style, everything these creepweasels hate?" She grins. "I wouldn't miss this for anything. Besides, I picked up a gross of misprinted pepper-spray keychains on a buy-nothing site. I'll just hand them out to anyone who wants one. Y'know, just in case."

She heads into the crowd on her errand. Jimi stays with us, fidgeting and glancing around.

"Jimi, what's the word?" I ask.

"It's 11:37 a.m., seventy-nine degrees."

"Any soundtrack news?"

He furrows his brow, listening to music only he can hear. "On this side of the street, I'm picking up themes of hope and community. Resistance. Across the way, it's creepily empty. I imagine that will change when the marchers get here."

The day grows warmer as noon approaches. Most of the counter-protesters were smart enough to bring water and wear sun hats. Other than the first-aid tent, the plaza is mostly unshaded in the middle of the day, but there are a few trees along the street. We gather under one.

"It's 12:02 p.m., eighty-two degrees," Jimi reports. "And I'm picking up a dire-sounding march."

All I hear is the tromp of many feet, along with shouted chants. The first marchers appear. They're all dressed in black, most in tight long-sleeved T-shirts. Lots of sunglasses but not one hat in the crowd. And quite a few bald heads, so I hope they remembered sunscreen. Or not. They all sport red armbands with the

HHH logo.

As they pass us on their way into the park, the Angry Aunties launch into a spirited rendition of "All You Fascists Are Bound to Lose." Hard to go wrong with Woody Guthrie.

But apparently these HHH dudes are music haters. A bunch of them come right up to the police tape on their side of the street, taunting the counter-protesters. Folks on our side move closer to the street, waving their signs. I turn toward the singers and crank up an invisible volume knob until they drown out the chanting. And then, just because I feel like it, I turn back and flip off the fascists. Three of them get a nicely contrasting splat of bird poop down the fronts of their black shirts. One of them, a guy with a neck tattoo, says something to his companions and takes off up the street, back along the route of the march.

A marcher stumbles and nearly falls near the police tape on our side. A deputy catches him and helps him sit on the curb. Dana is there almost instantly with a bottle of water. "I'm a nurse," she says. "Are you okay?"

The guy looks up—it's Tyler. "I don't feel so good."

"Probably dehydrated and overheated," she says. "Who thought it was a good idea to wear black on a sunny day? Come on, let's get you into the shade." She looks to Darrin for help. I go instead—Tyler hasn't seen Darrin over here on our side yet and doesn't know me. Together, we help Tyler up and support him to the first-aid tent.

"Taylor," he mumbles.

"We'll let her know," I assure him, and dash back out to tell Darrin.

The marchers fill the park in front of the Grand Stump stage, most standing but a few sitting under the trees. A warm-up speaker is shouting jokes and encouragement into the microphone, telling them how strong they are, not like those pussies across the street. Oh, how I want to birdshit the whole lot of them.

"I texted Taylor to come pick up her dude," Darrin says. "Mama Dana will stay with him till then."

"She's good people," I say. "I don't know if I would've been that nice."

"I think you would, but maybe only after a bird crap episode."

It's like he reads my mind.

The last of the marchers crowd into the park. I can't count them, but the numbers must be in the hundreds.

"Their march is drowning out almost everything else," Jimi reports. "But I'm picking up a theme of ... deception? And Barbara, your hero music is in a minor key."

"I'm scared," I admit. "We've never gone up against anywhere near these numbers." Some of whom might be armed. Ulp.

I turn my attention to the current speaker on the mic. What if they have their own mind-controller? Could that explain why so many ordinary guys are willing to be part of such a hateful organization? But I'm not feeling the telltale itch in my ears. These guys chose to be here.

Darrin chuckles. "I just sent some mosquitos and

wasps over to bug them. No stinging, for now."

Members of the HHH crowd dance around and swat at the insects, but no one makes a move to leave. The sound of an engine cuts into my awareness. An ambulance for Tyler? He didn't seem that bad off. Maybe it's Taylor. But wasn't the street closed?

An extra-large pickup accelerates and swerves onto the sidewalk, pointed straight at the Angry Aunties. Straight at Darrin.

I throw down the toughest force field I can manage. The truck hits it hard enough to deploy the air bags and kill the engine. As they deflate, the driver opens the door. He steps out, wobbles, and collapses to the ground. I recognize his tattoo. Before he can get up, I picture Mjolnir and set my foot on his chest, right on top of the bird splat.

"Just stay down and you won't get hurt," I say.

He spouts a nonsensical rant about woke commie lesbian anarchists but doesn't get far before a deputy steps up to arrest him. I remove my foot.

Another deputy approaches me. "Please step back, miss," she says. "We do not encourage private citizens to try to apprehend perpetrators."

"I acted without thinking. Probably won't happen again." No promises, though.

I look up and meet Tyler's gaze. He stands in front of the first-aid tent, clutching a half-empty water bottle and staring horrified at the truck and its driver. Maybe he's waking up to the reality of HHH.

A new speaker gets on the mic, and my ears begin to

itch as my brain actively rejects the mind-controlling voice of Matt Sherman.

"Brothers, thank you for allowing me to be part of this successful event. All of you strong, white men are capable of greatness."

Oh. No. Is this the deception Jimi heard? If so, Sherman has an army of hundreds of fit, angry men at his command, with a target right across the street. What do we have? Protest songs, wasps, bird crap, a gross of pepper spray keychains, and a guy who can tell us how hot it is. I doubt there's enough police presence here to keep a lid on things if they pop off.

"Don't let anyone say you are unworthy because of your white skin," Sherman continues. "You can be leaders in government, business, and the military. We need strong leaders in this country."

I fully expect him to tell them that they deserve to be those leaders, with everyone else below them. I could fly across and shut him up before he requests a specific action. But that would out me as a superhero in front of a hostile crowd.

"You know who else can be leaders?" Sherman asks. "Women. People of color. People with disabilities. I didn't used to think so, but queer folk." Bewildered muttering from the crowd, but no pushback. "Yes, you are capable of greatness. But not because of your skin. You are worthy. But not because of your penises."

A ripple of awkward laughter breaks the tension.

"Every human being is worthy of respect," Sherman says. "Maybe you are called to be a supportive follower of a leader who is different from you. That role has value. Listen to diverse voices and boost their signal in the realms where you command respect. Both groups will be better for it."

Okay, he really is our mind controller.

"No one is trying to replace you," he says. "They just want a share in what has always been available to you. People who are different from you are not your enemy. Your enemy is someone telling you what to think and how to act, as if there is only one way."

Is that what they call irony? But a lot of the marchers are taking off their armbands. Those near the park exit drift away from the rally, puzzled expressions on their faces.

"Who here is a billionaire?" No hands, but more laughter. "If you're struggling financially, you have more in common with other working people, no matter their identity, than you do with a billionaire. But it's not a zero-sum game. We all do better when we all do better."

Sherman is still talking to the shrinking crowd when Taylor runs up. Darrin points in Tyler's direction, but he is already on his way to meet her. They embrace.

"I'm so sorry, babe," Tyler says. "I've been an idiot with all this HHH stuff. It was like a cult or something. But I'm done with all that." He strips off his armband and drops it into a garbage can.

"That's good, because I'm still planning to go to law school," Taylor says.

"You'll be amazing," Tyler assures her. "I'm so lucky I get to marry you."

So, our mission today wasn't a battle. It was a rescue. I'm okay with that.

"What do you think?" I ask Darrin as they go off together. "Sherman's mind control will wear off after a few days if it isn't renewed. Is Tyler safely out of HHH, or will he relapse?"

"Hard to say," Darrin replies. "My gut says Tyler will be okay. The ones who were already haters might revert. But maybe the group will fall apart now."

"There's always another group," I say. "Like bindweed and blackberry, remember?" I look around at the counter protesters, still singing and joyfully waving signs. "But we're not gardening alone. Like our mission statement says, we'll keep weeding out evil and injustice wherever we find them."

Over Coffee

by Benjamin Gorman

Cassandra
why do you drink strong coffee
instead of whiskey or vodka
something numbing
anyway, I'm sure you know
he's promising mass deportations now
20 million people, he says
it doesn't take foresight to see
camps in the desert
millions dead
but no one else is panicking
some want it, this promised holocaust
some say it's not their biggest issue
some deny it
convinced it won't happen
I feel so alone in my fear

my mom said I should pray
to her god but
I've come to you
a mortal cursed with
perfect prophesy and never believed
I don't know the future
I know they are not scared enough
I feel like screaming myself hoarse
but I don't want whiskey or vodka
I need to see it happen
to know I'm sane
thanks for listening
Amen

Hatchling

by John Slovacek

20XX—Arleston, Texas:

Someone was screaming for help out in the hallway. Cinnamon Mathew StJames cowered alone in his apartment and did nothing.

He went by Cin these days. Long gone was the adventurous boy on the makeshift raft, charting a course down the Mississippi. Life and fear had claimed that part of him. He was a Louisiana Quarantine Zone refugee, one of the many orphans who survived those terrible years. He had done what he had to back then. He still bore the white scarring at the edges of his eyes that marked him forever as a survivor of the devastating Neverland virus.

Now an adult, Cin was paralyzed by his nerves and by the harshness of the city. Even worse, he was sure that he was sick with something new.

The woman in the hallway screamed again and fell silent. Cin held his breath. The respite was brief, replaced by the sounds of struggle and people shouting.

"Stop resisting!"

The trouble had started fifteen minutes before with raised voices several apartments down. From what Cin could tell, someone was being arrested. It must have gone wrong, because the event escalated into a physical conflict out in the hallway. He couldn't tell how many people were involved. Lots of them. Their voices were harsh and labored. Cin was certain he could hear blood splashing onto the concrete floor. He was frozen in his kitchen, dancing at the edge of a complete mental breakdown.

He had known from the beginning that the Military Police were involved. He could tell from the clack of their boots in the hallway before any of them had said a word. Cin was awful around MPs. He wore his panic like a big bright hat.

The scuffle outside moved closer. That familiar icy fear rose in him, like groundwater in the back of his throat. This was beyond normal anxiety; it was surely a symptom of this new disease. Not that he had any real way of knowing. Not like he could afford an answer. His heart pounded darkness into the backs of his eyes, and he itched badly from his scalp to his tailbone.

This is it, Cin thought. *This time the MPs will take me. I'll be just another disappearance.*

Rationally, he knew the odds of that were thin. He probably wasn't even on their radar any longer. They'd roughed him up on his way in earlier that day but let him pass. They didn't seem to know or care who he was. Not that he was anyone. He had no "special interest" affiliations that the authorities knew of. He kept to himself and had a steady job. They weren't interested in him. Right?

Cin tried to stop shaking.

Had it been this bad back before he moved to Arleston? No. That life seemed so long ago, like a movie starring someone else.

Arleston was its own world. Everyone knew it was awful, that was the whole shtick. It was different to **live** through it every day. Wading through that stifling haze of humanity and insidious foulness left him heavy, like he had absorbed it into his bones. The skyscrapers smothered the streets in delirious shadow, deepened by seasons of diseased rain.

Other people could live their lives normally. How?

Cin was on medication (when he could afford it). The drug was supposed to refocus his thoughts on things outside his crises, but it was rarely helpful. The side effects were unpredictable and left him exhausted and dizzy. He took his last two pills and waited. The brutality outside carried on. Cin twitched involuntarily with every sound. The fight was so close that an errant baton slammed hard against his door.

Cin's chest tightened. His fear tore at him with ragged fingernails. He made a desperate decision—the fearful action of an addict. He secured his Augmented Reality Goggles and activated the Belt at his hip. A menu screen flickered to life in front of his eyes and hung in the hazy air. Cin felt a familiar, hollow relief.

He fidgeted with the Belt, projecting out several screens at once. Two wellness blogs, some stand-up comedian, and a documentary.

The clinic psychiatrist had called this process 'Mental Saturation.' It was some new method out of the East Coast to treat anxiety for cheap. If life gets bad, just drown it out. Easier said than done under these conditions. Still, in its own way the method had helped him when things got bad. And things were especially bad. These newer symptoms—this manic fear and frenzy—they felt different. They unsettled him. Cin tried to explain this during his last session, but he had only been able to afford six minutes of therapy. The feed cut off at three.

Presently, Cin cursed. He had wanted a documentary about roads—something dull to settle the mood—but the AI had corrected it to 'toads'. *Again with the damn toads.* Arleston was infested with cane toads and had been for years. He hated their rattling croaks and the way they scampered across the sidewalk every morning.

The screens competed for volume.

The MPs would hear all this noise.

No. The thugs were busy enough.

A grim thought.

"Dahlia?"

"Always here, Cin," came her response.

Dahlia was the AI that Cin had chosen as his Belt assistant. She had been one of the possible free personalities built into the Belt's OS. Cin liked her okay. She could get cheeky.

"Dahlia, times are tough." He felt stupid and awkward saying it. "I need something relaxing to help my brain settle."

"You got it, boss."

A screen appeared dead center, a mandatory bank ad. The other screens politely fell silent.

A sickly man reclined in a hospital bed. A sinister doctor loomed over him, holding out a long slip of paper. The man in the bed pleaded and whimpered. No way he can afford that! Then, when all hope seemed lost, someone burst in through the door. He was scowling, caped, and dressed like a stack of hundred-dollar bills. He extended a hand.

"Yo! I'm Mr. Medical Loan!"

Without further explanation, the bank mascot hurled himself at the doctor and sucker punched him in the jaw.

Cin had seen this commercial before, his eyes already glazing over.

The ad gave way to a show already in progress. A trio of hulking gentlemen in matching outfits struggled to remain upright on the deck of a ship crossing turbulent seas. The camera backed out to show them teetering at the edge of a wave, threatening to capsize any second.

Back on the deck, one man turned to the other.

"Marv, I swear to you on my life, this season we're taking home maybe thirty humpbacks. What you think?"

The other man, Marv, turned to his fellow and belched.

The camera backed out again, this time with a venomous guitar lick.

"The Rango Brothers Versus Whales"

The image transitioned without warning to a bloody battle between a harpooned whale and the ratty whaling boat. Marv was thrown overboard. The whale bellowed.

The carnage was too much for Cin. He pulled the comment section up to shield his eyes from the video.

"Dahlia, why did you put this trash on?"

Morbidly curious, he checked the comments:

"Yeah! Fuck the Whales!"

"Is this legal now?"

"Gabafor said whales damaged the pipeline. Do not trust the shamestream media!"

"#GABAFOR"

"Marv is my baby daddy!"

Gabafor. Cin hated that guy. It wasn't a rare sentiment. He scratched the back of his neck aggressively and kicked the virtual screen away. The MPs in the hall must have called for backup. Fresh sets of boots rushed to join the fray. Cin hummed loudly against the noise, flipping open several more random videos. As a final touch he pushed the rickety Belt to its limit by projecting three multi-colored AR Corgies that danced absurdly around his feet.

The sounds of assault were muffled by loud, vapid nonsense. Cin finally stretched and relaxed his legs. He walked to the living room, further from the front door.

In an unfortunate coincidence of silence between the many floating programs, Cin heard a woman yelling something in the hall. It sounded like her face was smashed against the door.

Now he was sure who it was: the Aguilar family. He had helped Mrs. Aguilar take her groceries up a few times. He worried she'd think the behavior old-fashioned or forced, but she'd been so genuine and so grateful. He felt good afterwards, like a part of him had been healed.

What was happening? Was her family in the country illegally?

Did it matter?

He kept picturing those groceries.

She brought him a bowl of soup made with fava beans one evening. No reason. What was he doing to help her now?

He scoffed.

Maybe she was some kind of dissident. Maybe she committed some crime. Cin didn't know her or her family. He didn't need to help.

He didn't need to do anything.

Cin tapped a floating speaker, turning up the weather forecast until it made his ears throb.

"There's a genuine chance of even more rain across the city and south through the valley. We had a better one last year but, obviously, that's over. It was a real hot summer, and if the vapors we saw back in June are any indication, we can expect a much higher toxicity for these first couple weeks.

"As always, when you go out, assume it's gonna rain and assume it's dirty rain. Bring a real, proper umbrella and try to get to where you're going—"

Cin backhanded the screen's audio out of existence. Things were so bad that the weather channel sounded like a horror show. The corgis at his feet had started a conga line that felt disrespectful. Cin replaced them with more polite otters and sat down in the middle of the floor.

Outside the dusty window, it started raining. It slapped down in fat globs shining translucent yellow in the glaring sunset, painting the cloudy sky a sad ocher. The sound of the rain and the color of the light had a claustrophobia effect, like a yellow quarantine tent. Cin knew the rain was bad even before the sharp, smoky smell seeped through the window.

"Hey, cheer up, Cin. Here's a look at what's going on near you!" Dahlia morphed the weather program into a local news report.

The screen showed somewhere familiar: Gibson Plaza, a small park near Cin's train station. It was a dreary little green space encircled by brick apartment buildings and perpetually ill maple trees.

Some students from the university had held a protest earlier that day. They demanded answers regarding the political murders allegedly carried out by Gabafor in Hawaii last March.

Predictably, the pro-Gabafor counter-protesters swarmed the protestors armed with Augmented Reality psychological warfare and metal pipes. They flooded the field with screens of intense gore and hateful images. Presently, the news station superimposed the offensive AR images onto the scene, blurring them into pixelated clusters the color of meat and blood that danced around their creators as they bore down on the student protesters.

Meanwhile, the police stood idly by in full view of the cameras, indifferent to the violence.

Cin checked the comments, unable to help himself. The very first one read:

Burn the university down.

An upsetting number of commenters agreed.

Gabafor's tenure had fostered a militant anti-academia mentality. Cin's scalp prickled and itched. He thought about replying some defense. After all, he knew good people at that school. Instead, he closed the screen. No sense in creating a stressful situation for himself later. His face burned red, and he tasted bile.

He just wished he were better.

"Dahlia, I feel weird."

"Oh no... Let's try this one, then."

A new screen appeared like a black hole in reverse. It showed a night sky with the dark silhouette of juniper trees in the foreground. At first nothing changed. Then, bit by bit, a cluster of lights appeared. They were cold blue, like will o' wisps, hovering low in the distance. Their glow sent ghostly shadows across the desert. A moment later the lights jetted up into the sky in total silence.

A distorted voice kicked in as the video repeated:

"This footage was gathered recently near a certain facility in Del Rio, Texas. As you can see by the administration of Project Lavender, this video is authentic"

There was a flash. A frenzied series of green and purple data and graphs traced the contours of the video. The speaker continued: "I do not know how—"

"Oops," Dahlia said.

The screen shut off.

"What the hell? Bring it back!"

"It won't open. Too bad."

"Well, what is this Lavender thing?"

"Oh! A coincidence. This footage is from earlier today in Palm Beach, Florida."

The new screen showed a government luncheon. Two men were seated at a table laden with tiny sandwiches. The caption read: **Australian AI Researcher Ot Harvis presents Project Lavender to US Vice President, Ingo Beckerson**.

The researcher, Harvis, was speaking:

"Yes, thank you. Project Lavender is my baby, of course, but it was a massive group effort. It has to be. As you surely know, Project Lavender is an AI program capable of discerning truth and accuracy in ways other major programs can't or won't. Its efficacy at spotting lies, that is, images, videos, misinformation, is fast approaching 100%. Far beyond—"

"Truth, you say?"

The shuffle of media off screen stopped at once. Vice President Beckerson stood up from the table. His height was intimidating

"Truth? Ha!" He scoffed. "So now your little company comes here begging for handouts?"

"Sir, I don't think you recognize the scope of this. Over thirty countries have already—"

"Yeah, Poindexter? And who gets to choose what truth is? You? Some robot? Robots don't think, they just do what they're told. I see your game... Coming here with your lie machine!"

"Sir, we have data. So much data!" The researcher raised his hands.

"The nerve to lie to my face!" The vice president flipped the table. Sandwiches were flung into the air. A plate hit the camera, cutting the feed. The live comments kept ticking by below.

"Bet that was all AI."
"So so obvious."
"AI. Beckerson would never do that."
"Fuck project lavender."
"Fuck Australia."
"Communists."

Cin's face curled in disgust. How could people act like this? Madness licked at the edges of his consciousness.

Wait, had the video even been real?

He turned his face away from the luncheon comments and focused on the screen showing the stand-up comedian who was concluding some anecdote.

"So, I says to them," the camera panned close to the sweating man, "fuck your emu!"

Cin cringed away from it. The face on the screen was larger than life; he could see pores like greasy valleys. He moved to close the screen, but the picture froze.

"Dahlia, this is not relaxing."

"Oh, was that what we were doing?"

Another mandatory ad took dominion:

The screen focused on a street-side shrine for a little

girl. Months of thick, gray dust clung to its faded photographs and artificial petals. A child's voice began to sing:

"For memories that drag you down
And leave you in a bleak December
Please try our newest miracle
Which we have named Donotremember."

The video pulled back to reveal the singer to be the translucent spirit of a young girl. She floated through the dreary street and into a bright, over-saturated poolside barbecue crowded with people.

A blank voice carried on in the background:

"Talk to your doctor about Donotremember. Isn't it time to remove those memories keeping you from seizing the life you deserve?" It went on to whisper the drug's litany of side effects.

The ghost approached a woman with her same hair color. She tugged at her sleeve.

"Mama, I'm so cold. I miss you."

The woman looked around at the crowd, then down at the girl. She started laughing.

"Who are you? Hey, whose kid is this? Someone, come get your kid!"

Cin felt poisoned. Everything about the commercial was intentionally horrid. The guffawing crowd showed too many teeth as the ghost looked around with wide, desperate eyes. Cin slapped the window out of existence, his face an iron mask with every muscle screwed up tightly. The light in the room was brightening, burning his eyes.

A white screen was towering over him, scattering the others like cockroaches. It switched to a POV of someone rushing through a dim forest. The footage was shaky and amateurish. The only sound was their hurried footfalls on dry branches.

"I'm here," a woman's voice whimpered. "After my last video—I'm so sorry I worried you all. I said too much." She coughed back a sob. "They came to my house, but I was gone. God, it itches so bad. I'm tired, guys. I'm tired. Please I'm begging, if any of you feel the symptoms I was talking about... If any of you feel that same fear, just get word out. They can't stop all of us!"

There was a sudden bright burst of light. The woman on the screen screamed in recognition.

The screen closed without warning.

"Oops, looks like that one violates terms and conditions." Dahlia's tone was coy and playful. "Or whatever."

Cin waited for Dahlia's next gambit, her next disturbing screen, but she paused. Instead, she turned down the volume of all the screens one by one. The madness in the hallway became extremely audible. Cin could hear people being dragged towards the elevators. Among them were the shrill, panicked voices of two confused children.

Cin's vision darkened. He remembered the QZ, the

things that were done to them out there, the stink of the bodies left to rot in homes and manors across the bayou. He remembered Meta, who he had laid to rest in the swamp the night she was shot dead. The survivors, mostly children, had lived in constant danger within the fenced-in QZ, not just from virus or poverty, either.

Had anyone learned anything from the ravages of that pandemic? Now it seemed clear that some new disease had befallen them, but the major parties responsible for disease control were either long gone or hobbled. He wondered what other germs were running rampant. He scratched his neck and felt contaminated. His mouth tasted like the dirty rain. He felt old.

Out in the hallway, Mrs. Aguilar called for help one last time. The elevator door closed, and the voices were finally cut off. Cin was too late, as always. He retched through his teeth. A line of intense pain flared down the center of his scalp and down his spine. The weight of that cry tore him apart, and anger spilled out like blood.

Dahlia chirped.

A new screen rose up from the ground. It hung inches in front of Cin's face. He struggled to focus. On the screen, President Andre Gabafor himself—wide and bulbous, a toad masquerading as a man—stared disdainfully out onto a crowd of reporters.

"You there, with the hat."

"Mister President, please. We need answers about the disappearances. Many accounts point to the Military

Police. Do you have any statement?"

"What outfit are you with?"

A pause, total silence. Then:

"I'm with the Miskatonic Times, but—"

"Yeah, no wonder." Gabafor's tone was sinister and low. He jerked his head at his security. "Get that guy out of here."

Several burly agents shuffled out of frame to remove the man.

Gabafor turned back to the camera, staring directly into it, directly out at Cin.

"For all you real Americans, even though you didn't need to ask, of course the MPs aren't just 'taking people away.' People disappear all the time. Who cares? Grow up. This is just like the typical fucking media, excuse me..."

Gabafor made a rude gesture and turned away.

The video cut off, leaving only the comment section where fanatics and bots erupted in wild support of his new tirade. As if joining in with their revelry, the other screens regained their volume and boomed to life at once. Cin barely noticed.

How had they let it all get so far?

Because it was easy to just let it happen.

Easy to adjust to new realities and new injustices.

Cin remembered the vicious comments from the protest video. He remembered his own inaction even more clearly. He was too much of a coward to even do something meaningless. He couldn't even pretend properly.

God, was this all he would ever be?

Was this all he could do for the world?

He felt so pathetic. He tried to yell but coughed up a small spray of blood. He was rejecting himself like a bad organ. The screens flashed for attention while their speakers wailed a cacophony of voices and advertising jingles. The toad documentary was playing backwards. There must have been a screen buried beneath the others that somehow mimicked Mrs. Aguilar's screams. Cin was beyond wondering how this was possible. He seemed to be having auditory hallucinations. If not, then there were several more hidden screens playing videos of his late grandmothers screaming his name in fear. He covered his ears and looked down; the otter holograms had dissolved into legless toads that slithered around his feet like deranged maypole dancers.

He fell to his knees as pain overwhelmed him. He clutched at the back of his neck. The goggles suddenly felt extremely heavy.

Dahlia might have said a word just then, only it was spoken in a language Cin should not have known.

"Hatch"

Cin was hit with the dizzying feeling of being superimposed twice in the same location. As one Cin shrank in fear, succumbing to his weakness, a second, much larger Cin woke up inside him, but faced the opposite direction. His eyes stared at the back of his skull as his other eyes stared at the screens. The two shared one mind. Their skin was now painfully tight. With strong, broad nails like flat chisels, the stronger Cin began tearing his way out. He realized he had something like a hooked egg tooth that helped him quicken the labor. In moments, Cin was looking out with his own eyes at the freedom of the dark living room. He was now the only consciousness known as Cin.

With some effort, he pushed himself out through the tear he had created in what was once his spine. The air was especially cold on his nascent skin. It filled him with energy.

What had emerged from the husk was a thing entirely renewed. He was Cin in totality. He pulled himself across the floor of the living room with unnatural strength, although his skin was raw and new and stung against the ratty carpet. It didn't matter to him. All he could see was the door leading out to the hallway. Beyond it he could hear the vibrations of the building and, far below, the MPs taking the family away.

Maybe he would be quick enough, maybe not. His chin ended in a sharp, beak-like protrusion that he used to pull himself forward even faster. By the time the newborn Cin made it to the kitchen, he was moving with so much force that he blew the front door off its hinges and across the hallway. It didn't matter. He was truly alive and truly human—ascended—a super Id. He was a being of pure intent and action. He was following the sounds, racing along a river of condensed and directed anger.

Behind him, back in the dark living room, the Cin husk slowly deflated and folded over forwards. Its goggles hit the ground with a hollow crack, a spark, and a puff of smoke.

The next day, a team of government agents seized the apartment's security camera footage and data. However, over the years, instances of the gruesome, grainy footage would appear in certain corners of the internet. These leaks were typically removed within days. Their brief tenures amassed high traffic and pages of comments, which fell into predictable patterns:

"Bullshit."

"So fake"

"Wait, is this the thing they say went after Gabafor?"

"No, you dumb rube. It's AI. Santa Claus and leprechauns went after Gabafor. Stop believing everything you read online."

Definitions

by Jes Honard

What is freedom, anyway?
How do you define a word that lives in shadows?
A shapeshifter defined by the powerful to mislead the masses.

Today—today, freedom is kneeling on the bathroom floor,
a pregnancy test clutched in your hands.
Knowing it's too soon
and you're too young
but none of it matters.
Because the state you live in tells you the worst day of your life is a miracle.

It's huddling in terror, listening to the cries of your classmates as footsteps draw near.

Holding your breath,
texting your mom,
closing your eyes.
The thoughts and prayers that wash over your body are soaked in blood and dollar signs.

It's tentatively trying new pronouns, feeling more yourself than ever.
Embracing a new name,
a new wardrobe,
a new life.
Having it all stripped away because who you are is dangerous.
Who you are is wrong.

It's minimum wages tied to maximum expectations.
Work hard. No, harder.
Work fast. No, faster.
Get educated, accrue debt.
Fall behind checking the boxes you were told would get you ahead.

It's being told to bend yourself to today's version of success.
To close your eyes and smile as hatred falls like acid rain.
To look away and stay complicit even as they
abduct our protestors,
deport our neighbors,
eviscerate our jobs.

Freedom is watching the powerful respond with a shrug.
Freedom for who, you ask?
For everyone, they say.
So long as everyone looks like me.
Talks like me.
Thinks like me.
Believes like me.

So, what is freedom?
It's a bundle of false promises with a knife in its hand.
But it's also a call to arms.
For the queer and the Black
the immigrants and the disabled
the indigenous and the unhoused
the pregnant teenagers and the students buried in debt.
The middle-class families and the federal workers.
For everyone who is not the one percent of the one percent.

It's hope, buried in the soil of a world we're slowly letting burn.
Watering it with tears of frustration and anger and deciding,
despite it all,
to persist.

About the Authors

Chrys Gorman

(she/her) is a queer, neurodivergent booklover, guillotine aficionado, and co-owner of Not a Pipe Publishing. She currently lives in Barcelona, Spain with her husband, kid, three dogs, and two cats.

Rachel A. Rosen

(she/her) is an activist, graphic designer, and for her sins, a high school teacher. In a previous life, she published two long-running anarchist 'zines and designed the uniform for the Christie Pits Hardball League. She is the author of *Cascade*, the first book in *The Sleep of Reason* trilogy and its sequel, *Blight*. With Zilla Novikov, she is the co-author of *The Sad Bastard Cookbook: Food You Can Make So You Don't Die.*

Casey Aimer (he/him) is a science fiction poet and editor living in DC with his wife. He is founder of *Radon Journal*, an anarcho-sci-fi publisher. Most nights, you can find him planning direct action against fascists or at a local punk show, moshing as a form of therapy and community building—or hooking his brain up to computers and hoping the singularity would hurry up and arrive.

Kent Karnofski (he/him) is an emergent writer, image maker, and mathematician. He is the lead hooligan in all of his best dreams. He lives on the West Coast of the Americas. Find him at www.PlutoisFlat.com

Benjamin Gorman (he/him) is an award-winning former high school English teacher, political activist, author, poet, and publisher at Not a Pipe Publishing. He's an author-in-exile living in Barcelona, Spain with bibliophile and guillotine aficionado Chrys, their kid Franke, three dogs, and two cats. His novels are *The Sum of Our Gods*, *Corporate High School*, *The Digital Storm*, and *The Convention of Fiends* series beginning with *Don't Read This Book* and continuing in *You Were Warned.* He's also the author of two books of poetry, *When She Leaves Me* and *This Uneven Universe,* and the non-fiction book *Dear America: A Breakup Letter*.

Joanna Michal Hoyt (she/her) is a community volunteer, farmer, baker, and writer who tries stubbornly to see and serve God in everyone. Having grown up in a conservative Christian homeschool group and a progressive unschool group, she knows and loves people on multiple sides of the country's deep divides. She's lived and worked with

communities that farmed sustainably, welcomed refugees and migrants, and tried to help neighbors in rural New York State and rural Georgia, and now she lives and works at a Massachusetts farm which is also a residential treatment center for adults dealing with major mental illnesses. Read more of her speculative and historical fiction, often preoccupied with faith, fear, the edges of rationality and the things that connect us across divides, through links from https://joannamichalhoyt.com/

Julia Figliotti

(she/her) is a poet, singer-songwriter, and published author living in Western New York with her husband, cats, and reptiles. When she's not hunched over a notebook or making up melodies, Julia justifies her existence in a world determined to equate production and worth by soil toiling in other people's gardens, reading trivia for high school quiz bowl competitions, and performing in a kick-ass Fleetwood Mac tribute band. Her dream is to attract the interest of a wealthy patron, who will fund her passion for creating poetry and music that reaches into the human experience and pulls out the guts for all to see.

A.M. Pennyfeather (she/her) is an author, mom, and wife. Her life revolves around her family, especially her young daughter, but stories about the truest of loves energize her heart. When she's not making up her own worlds—or enjoying someone else's—she's probably spending time with her family, often in the beauty of nature.

Brian U. Garrison (he/him) writes for children, adults, and grand adults. His writing reflects the stories that he reads: poetry, science fiction and fantasy, a smattering of just-plain-ol'-science, joke books, and so much more. When he's not writing or reading, he loves climbing trees, digging in the garden, and learning new chords on his ukulele (and banjolele). He'll happily sign your copy of his chapbook *New Yesterdays, New Tomorrows* if you find him ordering Thai curry from his favorite food cart in Portland, Oregon.

Christopher Scott Thompson (he/him) is the author of *The Book of Onei* and *If In Ruins We Must Live*, published by Ritona Press, and of *Pagan Anarchism*, published by Gods and Radicals. His poems have appeared in several publications, including *Gods and Radicals* and *A Beautiful Resistance*.

Trixie Belka was born with an old soul, and soon after, realized the world wasn't fair. She set out to make her corner of it more so. #NotAllPaladinsWieldSwords

Kurt Newton (he/him) has been writing poetry for most his adult life, some even earlier. His poem "Koala Bear Underwear" in the fifth grade was a big hit among classmates. His interest in politics goes way back to before he was born. His mother was a volunteer on the campaign to elect John F. Kennedy. Kurt's more recent political commentaries can be found in *More Alternative Truths*, *Alternative Truths: Endgame* and at *Eye to the Telescope*. His writing life (among other things) is on display at Facebook. Send him a friend request; he could use it.

Stephanie Carrier-Boodram (she/her) is a multidisciplinary artist from Montreal. She studied in design and cinema. Her stories weave connections between the visible and the invisible, opening doors to untold realities. Inspired by nature and her two children, her work sparks curiosity and touches the heart.

J. L. Henker

(she/her) is a fantasy/sci-fi author, blogger, and host of the *Women Fantasy Authors* YouTube channel. Her career includes stints as a bookseller and used book buyer. She lives in northern California with her partner Diane and a ginger cat with attitude named Leo. When not writing, you'll find her collecting vintage recipes, haunting thrift shops, and hiking in northern California's amazing regional, state, and national parks.

Madeline White

(she/her) is a queer author, farmer, artist, and anarchist currently traveling the country in a converted box truck. Her published works include those in *Honeyguide Magazine* (Issue 8), *Cowboy Up* by WolfSinger Publications, and *Howling For You* and *Sincerely, Departed* by Voices from the Mausoleum. In her free time, she works to build community and resistance, and writes hopeful stories about the collapse of the world as we know it.

M. K. Martin (she/her) is an author and editor. Her work appears in literary journals, in several anthologies, and in her novels *Survivors' Club*, *Ashfall*, and *New Avalon Rangers* (available May 2025). Martin is a restless world traveler who started writing young. She was an exchange student to Paraguay, joined the US Army, got deployed to Afghanistan and to Iraq, and currently lives in Ireland where she indulges her deep love of tea. Find out more at mkmartinwriter.com

Desiree Batiste (she/her) is an author whose works appear in many literary journals such as *Fine Lines Magazine*, *Impspired*, *The Rye Whiskey Review,* and the *Lothlorien Poetry Journal.* She has also self-published two poetry compilations titled, *The Shaping of a Diamond* (Dec.

2022) and *Shimmering Brilliance* (Oct. 2023). *The Shaping of a Diamond* tells Batiste's journey as a survivor of child abuse and domestic violence and is a very raw and inspiring introspective told through poetry. Suffering from PTSD, depression, panic attacks, and anxiety as the result of her past trauma, Batiste uses her writing therapeutically and hopes to connect with others in similar circumstances to let them know they are not alone. She is married, with an adult son and daughter and six cats. Find out more at: www.authordesireebatiste.com

Rick M. Cook

(he/him) Rick is a speculative fiction author living in Beaverton, Oregon. His dream of providing a home for ten thousand dogs has been put on hold pending an HOA review. Until then, he remains a retired software engineer/consultant and lover of science fiction & fact. He's a member of Willamette Writers, working on his SFWA membership, and has published stories in the anthologies *The Phone* (editor: J. Komp) and *Stories (Within)* (editor: Benjamin Gorman). His claim to fame? Having worked on the

Kepler Space Telescope, various automotive & spacecraft worldwide, and seeing the James Webb Space Telescope in person. Find him at https://linktr.ee/rickmcook

Karen Eisenbrey (she/her) lives in Seattle, WA, where she leads a quiet, orderly life and invents stories to make up for it. She's the author of the *Daughter of Magic* trilogy (*Daughter of Magic*, *Wizard Girl*, and *Death's Midwife*), the *St. Rage* series (*The Gospel According to St. Rage*, *Barbara and the Rage Brigade*, and *Far from Normal*), *Ego & Endurance*, and *Tales From Deep River, Book 1: A Quest for Hidden Things*. She also sings in a church choir and plays drums in a garage band. Find more info on Karen's books and short fiction, follow her band-name blog, and sign up for her quarterly newsletter at kareneisenbreywriter.com

John Slovacek

(he/him) (known online as Dead Carcosa) is an artist and writer specializing in horror, dreams, and the occult. He wrote and illustrated *Ghost City Stories* and has a story included in the anthology *The Magic We Miss.*

Jes Honard

(they/she) is an award-winning, queer author whose novels and short stories span the genres of fantasy, science fiction, and horror. Their work explores concepts of identity, trust, and belonging. Jes currently lives in Michigan with their wife and two cats.

www.ingramcontent.com/pod-product-compliance
Lightning Source LLC
Chambersburg PA
CBHW070451200726
48293CB00007B/2166

* 9 7 8 1 9 5 6 8 9 2 6 4 2 *